Gerard Karlshoven Gude

Armature of Helicoid Landshells

Gerard Karlshoven Gude

Armature of Helicoid Landshells

ISBN/EAN: 9783337392314

Printed in Europe, USA, Canada, Australia, Japan

Cover: Foto ©Andreas Hilbeck / pixelio.de

More available books at **www.hansebooks.com**

ARMATURE OF HELICOID LANDSHELLS;

AND A NEW SPECIES OF CORILLA.

BY G. K. GUDE, F.Z.S.

THAT Mollusca have numerous enemies is a fact well known to naturalists, for not only do they serve as food for many mammals, birds and reptiles, but they are preyed upon by some insects, and even by other mollusca. Naked slugs are especially exposed to the attacks of birds, slow-worms and snail-slugs (*Testacella*); and, in foreign countries, of carnivorous snails, such as *Glandina* and others. Shell-bearing Mollusca likewise are devoured by birds and mammals; they have besides many insect enemies, particularly under tropical climates, and we shall, therefore, not be surprised to find that in several instances these creatures have come to be provided with special means of protection. This has been attained in various ways, indirectly by protective resemblance between the forms or colours of the shells and their immediate surroundings; or, directly, by special structures, such as teeth, plates, or constrictions, serving as buttresses or barricades behind which the animal can withdraw. It is probable, however, that these structures may at the same time help to strengthen and support the outer wall of the shell, and in this manner safeguard the mollusc against injuries, accidental or otherwise.

In the following notes I propose to consider the several special structures or forms of armature, just indicated, as they are found in many of the genera of Helicidae, which have come under my notice. It will, of course, be understood that the operculum, which is so generally present in marine mollusca, and in the land and freshwater shells taxonomically associated with them, and the clausilium or elastic door, which characterizes and gives its name to the well-known genus of land-shells *Clausilia*, are also means of protection; but they do not form an integral part of the shell, and I do not propose to consider them here. A point to be noticed with regard to the armatures under consideration is that they are not the exclusive property of any particular genus, or wider group, but occur in various genera or groups, often of distant affinity.

I. CORILLA.

The Helicoid genus *Corilla*, with which we are concerned in the first place, is an interesting group of landshells inhabiting the jungles of Ceylon, with a single outlying species in the southern point of the Indian Peninsula. The armature, which sometimes exhibits considerable complication, consists generally of a variable number of revolving plates or folds on the inner side of the shell-wall. It may be mentioned as a curious fact that a single species, namely *Corilla charpentieri* (Ceylon), is devoid of armature (fig. 1).

I was favoured not long ago by Mrs. R. S. Fry, of Singapore, with some shells collected by

Fig. 1.—*Corilla charpentieri.*

her during a stay of several months in Ceylon; amongst these were eight specimens of a shell which, at first, I was inclined to refer to *Corilla odontophora*, of Benson, but, after some research and careful comparison with allied forms, it became evident that I had to deal with a new form. It is probable, however, that it already exists in collections, as Mr. Hugh Fulton sent me a specimen labelled

Corilla humberti, and Mr. John Ponsonby also possesses specimens of a similar form under the same name ; but on submitting one of my specimens to the describer of that species, Dr. A. Brot, of Geneva, he informed me at once that it was not *Corilla humberti*, but rather, he thought, a variety of *Corilla erronea*, of Albers. Dr. Brot obligingly forwarded one of the only two specimens of *Corilla humberti* known to exist in collections, so that, thanks to his kindness, I am enabled to give a figure of it for comparison with its allies.

There appears to be a certain amount of confusion with regard to the limits of some species, as well as to the position and number of teeth or plates in some of the Cingalese members of the genus, and it is hoped that the present notes may help to elucidate some of the doubtful points. The new shell is certainly distinct from all the published species of the group, and I have

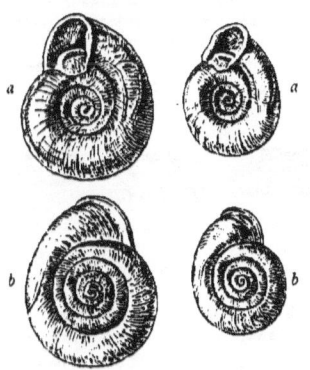

Fig. 2.—*Corilla fryae.* Fig. 3.—*Corilla erronea.*

much pleasure in associating with it the name of the lady to whose kindness I am indebted for this valuable addition to my collection.*

* *Corilla fryae*, n. sp.—Testa late umbilicata, ovato-rotundata, discoidea, solidula, rufo-castanea, planulata. oblique costulata, subtus valde concava, striata, pernitida ; spira plana, sutura vix impressa. Anfr. 5 vix convexiusculi, inter suturam et peripheriam valde angulati, ultimus subtus ornatur striis spiralibus quae secundum latus lineis vel rugis impressis obliquis decussantur ; antice convexior, valde dilatatus, profunde descendens. Apertura obliqua, obtuse subcordata. lamellis 3 parietales (media elongata, validaque, laterales minores, profundaeque). 4 palatales flexuosae, longulae, perlucentes, 3 ab apertura visibiles. Peristoma ex albido purpurescens vel rufo-castaneus, callosum valde reflexum, margo superior sub-dentate crassior, inferior dente valido alquae quadrato armatur.—Diam. maj. 26, min. 20, alt. 8 mm. Hab.—Albion Estate, Lindula District, Ceylon.

Corilla fryae differs from *Corilla erronea* (compare figs. 3*a* and 3*b*) in being more rounded in outline, larger, darker in colour and more shining beneath, the ribs are more regular and less coarse ; the whorls are less convex, almost flattened and distinctly angulated, almost keeled, midway between the suture and the periphery, while the suture is less impressed ; the last whorl is more constricted, and suddenly widens towards the aperture, becoming again constricted behind the peristome, and it is more deeply deflected in front ; the mouth is much less oblique, the palatal folds are longer and

Several of the specimens being more or less weatherworn, I had the less compunction in breaking away parts of the walls at various points, so as to examine their internal structure thoroughly, and to report thereon with precision. To enable the reader to understand the following remarks, I will here mention that those teeth or plates found on the inner wall of the shell are known as *parietal*, while those on the outer wall are called *palatal*.

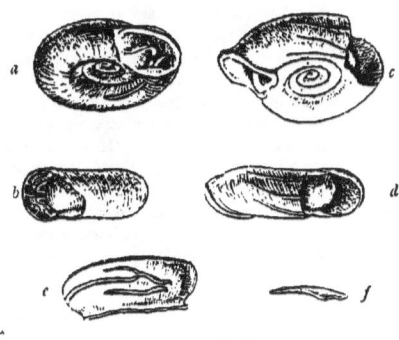

Fig. 4.—*Corilla fryae.*

In fig. 4*a*, the parietal plates are shown on the left and the palatal on the right of the aperture ; the figure shows a perfect shell of *Corilla fryae*. To the left of the aperture the median plate will be observed reaching outwardly up to the extreme margin of the parietal callus, while the tips only of two other plates, one on each side of the median, can be discerned. I propose to designate them by numerals, and, beginning at the top of the shell, the first will of course be No. 1, the median No. 2, and the next No. 3. In fig. 4*b*, a part of the outer wall has been removed, and the edge thus exposed is shown perpendicularly to the line of sight ; here on the right the curved and revolving parietal plates Nos. 1 and 3 show their inner terminations, while a reference to fig. 4*e* will explain why parietal plate No. 2 is invisible in the former figure, as it terminates at about half the length of Nos. 1 and 3, and there unites with the former. To return to fig. 4*b*, on the left four palatal plates will be observed, which will be numbered 1, 2, 3 and 4 respectively, from the top of the shell downward

It will be noticed that No. 1 curves upwards towards the shell-mouth (not shown in the figure), while No. 2 interlocks between the parietal teeth Nos. 1 and 3, and as it curves upwards towards the

more flexuous, and the tooth on the basal edge of the peristome is longer and more quadrate ; in this latter respect, as well as in contour and shape, the new shell more resembles *Corilla odontophora*. The specimens were all collected on the edge of a jungle where a new clearing was being made, on the Albion Estate, Lindula District, Ceylon (figs. 2, 4, 5, 6).

mouth, following for some distance the curvature of the second parietal plate, it is almost in juxtaposition with the latter; the third palatal plate also curving upwards, terminates below the third parietal one which curves downwards, and they therefore cross each other about the middle; No. 4 is situated very low down, close to the junction of the outer with the inner wall, and proceeds in an almost horizontal direction. These palatal plates are distinctly visible externally through the shell, and they are thus shown in figs. 4c and 4d, the latter figure exhibiting Nos. 1, 2 and 3, while the former shows Nos. 2, 3 and 4. The specimens delineated in figs. 2 and 4 are all mature, and as in this condition they are composed of 5 whorls, it follows that the plates are placed near the end of the fifth whorl. In fig. 4f the palatal plate No. 2 is shown by itself, the upper convex line indicating its attachment to the shell-wall. An interesting fact was revealed by the examination of an immature specimen received with the others; on breaking away the walls at various points, five palatal plates were observed in the fourth whorl, at a point which would be intersected by a line from the apex of the shell to the

and laminae of the Pupidae, observed that "they may answer the purpose of an operculum to keep out enemies, while they afford no obstacle to the motions of the soft and yielding body of the animal" ("Zoological Journal," iv., 1829, p. 168, footnote). As illustrating the vulnerability of unarmed shells, it may be mentioned that Jeffreys found a half-grown specimen of *Helix strigella* containing the larvae-form pupa of *Drilus flavescens*, the female of which has been named *Cochleoctonus vorax* from its snail-eating habit. He also found a similar pupa in a *Helix incarnata*, which, as in the case of *Helix strigella*, completely occupied the spire of the shell, of which it had devoured the former inhabitant ("Annals and Magazine of Natural History" (3), vi, 1860, p. 348). Of much interest is a note by Lt.-Col. Godwin Austen, who, in a paper on the Asiatic landshell genus *Plectopylis*, states that "when breaking up a number of shells to expose the barriers and ascertain if their characters were constant, I was greatly interested to find in two instances the presence of small insects that had become fixed between the teeth." He further remarks that those shells possessing such bars to the predatory visits of insects, such as

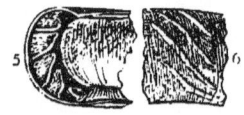

Figs. 5 and 6.—*Corilla fryae*, immature × 2.

Fig. 7.—*Corilla erronea*.

point where the plates would be found in the mature shells. This specimen is represented in figs. 5 and 6. On reference to fig. 5 it will be seen that the upper four of these plates are much broader than those of the mature shells, as they reach nearly to the inner wall and overlap, being placed close together, slanting upwards, but scarcely curving; No. 5 is very short and narrow, and corresponds in position to No. 4 in the older shells; fig. 6 shows the upper four plates in their immature position as seen through the shell. No plates being found in the fourth whorl of the mature shells, the inference is that as the shell is completed the plates first formed are absorbed by the animal, and this fact supports the view that the plates form barriers to exclude predatory insects. It may also be assumed that the animal produces similar plates from an early stage of its existence, absorbing them as each successive whorl with its complement of plates is completed; but this of course can only be demonstrated by the examination of a series of shells in various stages of growth. That structures of this kind serve as a means of defence was suggested as long ago as 1829 by Guilding, who, in speaking of the teeth

certain kinds of beetles, ants, or even leeches, all of which swarm in the forests where the shells are found, would have the best chance of surviving. ("Proceedings of the Zoological Society of London," 1874, p. 611.)

In fig. 7b, a portion of the inner side of the outer wall of the allied species, *Corilla erronea* (Ceylon), is shown with the plates *in situ*, disposed in much the same manner as in *Corilla fryae*; they are, however, shorter and less curved; the parietal plates are almost identical in position and shape with those of *Corilla fryae*, as shown in fig. 7a, but they are shorter and the union of Nos. 1 and 2 is not so complete. Fig. 7c shows a specimen sideways, which is of interest on account of a small adventitious tooth between palatal plates Nos. 2 and 3.

In figs. 8a and 8b *Corilla rivolii*, of Deshayes (Ceylon), is delineated, the latter figure showing the remarkably reflected lip, and the three parietal plates, of which Nos. 1 and 3 are much more exserted than in the two previously-mentioned species; the palatal plates also reach much nearer to the edge of the lip than in the other two species, but they are not shown in the figure, as the mouth of the shell was turned too far to the left. Fig. 8*a* shows the same shell with part of the outer wall removed, from which it will be seen that the arrangement of the plates is similar to that in *Corilla fryae* and *C. erronea* ; there is, however, what appears to be a small adventitious palatal plate or tooth between Nos. 3 and 4, but this was not found to be constant in other specimens of this species which I examined, and it may therefore be assumed that this is an abnormal case. Since writing the above, Mr. Ponsonby has kindly placed at my disposal two immature specimens of *C. rivolii*, the examination of which bears out the statement already made, that plates are formed at the various stages of growth, which are afterwards absorbed. These two specimens are shown in figs. 9*a*-9*f*, of which *a*-*e* exhibit one with four whorls completed, having five palatal plates, which resemble those of *Corilla fryae* (figs. 5 and 6) in being different in character from the mature plates. Here again they are much broader, they are also seen to be triangular, to overlap and to reach almost to the inner wall; no parietal plates are present. In fig. 9*a* the palatal plates are shown as seen on looking into the aperture, in fig. 9*b* they are looked at more from below, the shell being tilted a little. In figs. 9*c* and 9*d* they are shown as seen externally through the shell-wall. In fig. 9*e* the same specimen is depicted, seen from above, the dagger indicating the place

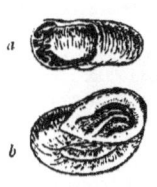

Fig. 8.—*Corilla rivolii.*

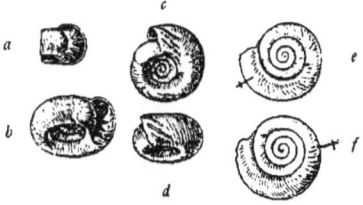

Fig. 9.—*Corilla rivolii* immature.

where the plates are found. Fig. 9*f* shows another immature specimen, the dagger here also indicating the position of the plates ; but while in the former specimen they are placed at the end of the fourth whorl, they are here found at a place where only three and-a-half whorls have been completed. Lt.-Col. H. H. Godwin Austen, in a letter, confirms my surmise as to the temporary character of these plates, stating that those found in the old shells differ very much from what those found in

the young might be supposed to develop into. He thinks that the early folds are absorbed to make way for subsequent ones. As will be seen from the consideration of *Corilla odontophora* further on, however, this is not always the case, since in one mature specimen I have found the immature palatal folds still existing.

Corilla odontophora does not seem to be well understood, and the figure given in Tryon's "Manual of Conchology" (2), iii., t. 33. f. 34, copied from Hanley and Theobald's "Conchologia Indica," t. 57, f. 6, is somewhat misleading, as it evidently represents an immature specimen, showing the palatal folds as they appear from the aperture, but no reference is made to this fact. Mr. Ponsonby having in his possession two mature specimens, which he doubtfully referred to this species, kindly permitted me to open one, which is shown in figs. 10*a*—10*e*. On reference to fig. 10*b* it

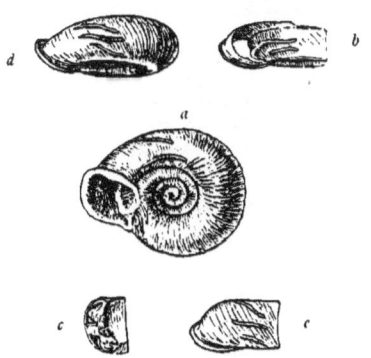

Fig. 10.—*Corilla odontophora.*

will be seen that only two parietal folds are present, corresponding to Nos. 2 and 3 in the previous species. Fig. 10*c* exhibits the plates as seen from behind their inner terminations, and it will be observed that there are four palatal folds, the upper three of which are shown through the wall of the shell in figs. 10*d* and 10*e*, while fig. 10*a* shows the entire shell from below (restored), with plates Nos. 3 and 4 showing through. On comparison with the figures of *Corilla erronea* and *Corilla fryae*, it is seen that in *Corilla odontophora* the palatal folds are much shorter and less flexuous than in the two former, and, as correctly stated by Benson in describing this species ("Annals and Magazine of Natural History " (7), xvi, 1865, p. 175), they "are entirely visible from the aperture." Another point to be noted is that the outer terminations (*i.e.* nearest the aperture) of the upper three palatal folds form an oblique line parallel with the peristome, the first one being nearest the aperture, while in *Corilla* *erronea* and *Corilla fryae* they form a semicircle, the second fold being nearest the aperture. The shell of *Corilla odontophora* is more regularly and less coarsely ribbed than that of *Corilla erronea*, and larger, although composed of only 4–4½ whorls, while the other two species have 5 whorls; it differs further from *Corilla erronea* in that the last whorl is more deflected in front, more tumid, and then suddenly contracted behind the peristome, more resembling *Corilla fryae* in these respects, as also in the presence of a quadrate tooth on the basal margin of the peristome. Before concluding the consideration of this species, I would draw attention to fig. 10*a*, in which, though the shell is adult, is seen the immature form of palatal folds immediately behind the callus of the mouth, and, as already mentioned, a circumstance which shows that the earlier folds are not invariably absorbed on the completion of the shell.

Fig. 11.—*Corilla humberti.*

Corilla humberti, also Cingalese, is extremely rare in collections. As Benson, in the paper cited above, throws some doubt on the correctness of Dr. Brot's figure of this species in the "Journal de Conchyliologie," xii., 1864, t. 2, f. 6, I was pleased to be able to give a new figure of it, and I am in a position to confirm Benson's conjecture that the original figure is slightly misleading, as the basal palatal fold appears to be joined to the suture owing to the position in which the specimen was placed, but on tilting the shell from the left side the fold is plainly seen to be unconnected with the suture, and it is thus shown in my fig. 11; this fold corresponds in position with No. 4 of the other species, while the parietal fold corresponds with No. 2 of the others. The specimen having been completely cut in half through the median plane, a close examination of the parietal fold reveals a slight fracture, and the inference forces itself upon my mind that, probably, in the process of cutting, it was partly cut away, and that it reached further back than it now appears. This form differs from the species already considered in having only one palatal and one parietal fold; it is also decidedly more rounded in outline, but like *Corilla odontophora* and *Corilla fryae*, it has a quadrate, but less elongate, tooth on the basal margin of the peristome.

The other species of *Corilla* will be considered in a future communication.

(*To be continued.*)

ARMATURE OF HELICOID LANDSHELLS.

By G. K. Gude, F.Z.S.

(Continued from page 92.)

IN my last article, in speaking of *Corilla humberti,* I stated that only two specimens were known to me to exist in collections, and that these were in the possession of Dr. Brot, who described the shell. Since writing, however, Mr. Ponsonby has shown me a specimen, which, upon being opened, proved to pertain to that species, although it is considerably less rounded in outline. The palatal tooth corresponds in size and position to that in Dr. Brot's shells, but the parietal fold extends much further back, a fact which confirms my surmise that this fold in the shell figured by Dr. Brot (and by me, fig. 11, *ante* p. 92) had been damaged in the cutting process. Colonel Beddome has informed me that he possesses three specimens of this species, which he has obligingly sent to me for inspection; one of these agrees with Mr. Ponsonby's shell in being somewhat oblong, while the other two conform to Dr. Brot's types as regards outline. The species certainly appears to be less rare than was at first supposed, and it may turn up in other collections.

We have now dealt with *Corilla charpentieri, C. fryae, C. erronea, C. rivolii, C. odontophora,* and *C. humberti.* The only other species of the genus at present known, are *C. anax,* Benson, and *C. beddomeae,* Hanley.

The two species last named, with which we are here concerned, form a separate group in the genus, and, from considerations which will be explained further on, may be looked upon as being the oldest members of the group provided with plates, *Corilla charpentieri* being the primordial form. This group of *Corilla anax* (including *C. beddomeae*), is of equal value to the group of *Corilla erronea* (including *C. fryae, C. rivolii, C. odontophora* and *C. humberti*) and to the remaining group of *Corilla charpentieri.*

Corilla anax is shown in figs. 12*a-e,* the drawings having been made from a specimen in Mr. Ponsonby's collection. It is the only species of *Corilla* known to occur outside Ceylon, being found, as already stated, in the southern part of India. It is of a dark chocolate colour, and possesses three parietal and four palatal plates.

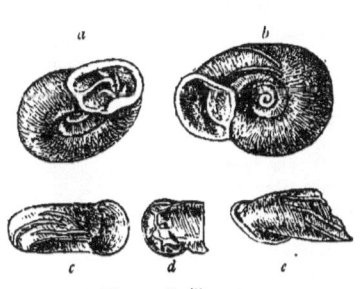

Fig. 12.—*Corilla anax.*

Fig. 12*a* shows the entire shell, four of the plates, two parietal and two palatal, being visible from the aperture. The parietal plates are much broader than in the other species, No. 1 curves upwards, while No. 2 reaches as far as the parietal callus; but, unlike those of the other species, they are separate. No. 3 parietal plate is almost horizontal, with but a slight curve, as will be seen on reference to fig. 12*c,* the specimen being there figured with the outer wall removed. Fig. 12*d* shows the same shell with part of the outer wall broken away, and the plates are shown as they appear from behind their inner terminations. The palatal plates also are seen to be much broader than in the other species, and the three upper ones are much more oblique, resembling in this respect the immature plates found by me in three of the other species. In fig. 12*e* a portion of the last whorl is drawn, in which the palatal plates Nos. 1, 2 and 3 are shown as they appear through the shell, while fig. 12*b* shows the entire shell from below with palatal plates Nos. 3 and 4 shining through. Colonel Beddome has been so good as to lend me several adult examples of this species for examination, one of which is of interest from the fact that it exhibits, in addition to the mature armature, immature plates which are identical in form and position with those I found in an adult shell of *Corilla odontophora,* and described in my previous article (*ante* p. 92). With these adult examples was an immature shell with three whorls completed, which is specially noteworthy in that it possesses two sets of immature plates, one near the end of the third whorl, and the other a little beyond the place where two and a-half whorls have been completed. It may therefore safely be inferred that the plates are not absorbed till after completion of the new ones, and it will be remembered that this is not an isolated case, for, as already stated, two sets of plates were observed by me in a full-grown specimen of *Corilla odontophora,* and Colonel Beddome lent me a shell of this last-named species, identical in this respect. Colonel Beddome informs me that he collected his specimens of *Corilla anax* on

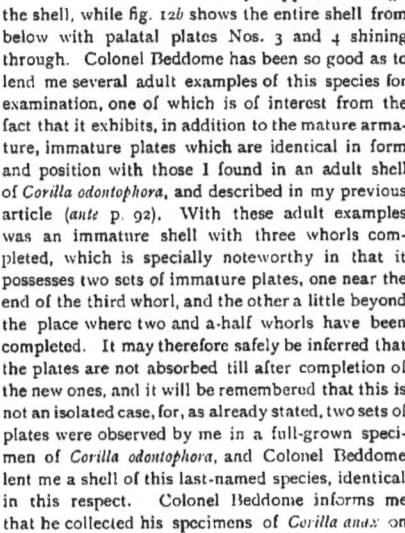

the Anamali Hills, in the Coimbatore District of South India, in moist woods, at 2,000 feet elevation, where it was very abundant on and under dead logs.

Corilla beddomeae (figs. 13 and 14*a-e*), is, I believe, somewhat rare in collections. Mr. Pilsbry has not included it in his synopsis of *Corilla* ("Manual of Conchology," ix., p. 147), but, guided probably by its external characters, he refers it to the genus *Plectopylis* (see Errata, Index, p. 121, of the same work). The absence of

Fig. 13.—*Corilla beddomeae*, type.

vertical or transverse barriers on the parietal wall, however, amply warrants its inclusion in the present genus. The species differs in appearance from the others in being wrinkled, thinner in texture and much flattened above. Fig. 13 shows the type from Haycock Mountain, Ceylon, the specimen being in Colonel Beddome's collection. It will be noted that it is strongly and regularly wrinkled, the rugae being particularly coarse above and about the keel, gradually decreasing towards the base. The specimen measures twenty millimetres in diameter. In figs. 14*a-e* a small variety from Wata-wala, Ceylon, is shown from a specimen kindly lent by Mr. Ponsonby, who, with his usual courtesy,

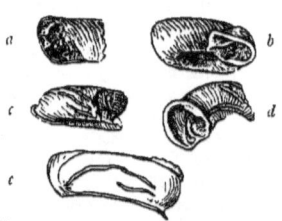

Fig. 14.—*Corilla beddomeae*, small variety.

allowed me to open the shell, although it was his only specimen. It will be noticed that this variety is less coarsely wrinkled than the type; it is also paler and smaller, measuring only sixteen millimetres in diameter. Fig 14*e*, which shows the shell with the outer wall broken away, discloses the fact that only two parietal plates are present, corresponding to Nos. 2 and 3 in those species possessing three plates; for the sake of uniformity they will be numbered 2 and 3; both are visible from the aper-

ture (see fig. 14*b*). No. 2 reaches to the parietal callus, and, as will be observed, it is long and irregularly flexuous, while No. 3 is very short. Of the four palatal plates Nos. 1 and 2 only are visible from the aperture. Nos. 1, 2 and 3, are broad, and ascend obliquely, parallel to each other, while No. 4 is smaller, narrower, and revolves horizontally, parallel to the suture, as may be seen on reference to fig. 14*c*, which shows plates Nos. 1, 2 and 3 shining through, and fig. 14*d*, which shows Nos. 2, 3 and 4. Fig. 14*a* shows all six plates from behind their inner terminations.

Fig. 15.—*Corilla charpentieri, var. hinidunensis.*

Colonel Beddome has also favoured me with the loan of specimens of a shell sent out by Mr. H. Nevill, under the name of *Corilla hinidunensis,* and published by him without description in "Enumeratio Heliceorum et Pneumonopomorum insulae Ceylon adhuc detectorum" (1871), p. 1. Mr. Pilsbry, in figuring this form in the ninth volume of the "Manual of Conchology," p. 148, t. 41, ff. 23–25, has, with his usual discrimination, reduced it to a variety of *Corilla charpentieri*, Pfeiffer, and a careful comparison of the two forms has convinced me that this view is the correct one, as the only difference which could be detected is that of size, *Corilla charpentieri* measuring twenty-nine millimetres, and Nevill's *Corilla hinidunensis* twenty-two millimetres. To complete the series I have thought it useful to add a figure of

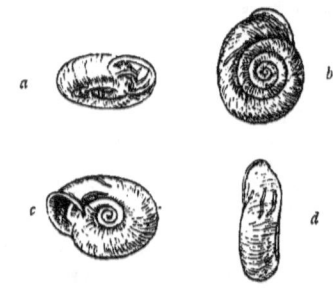

Fig. 16.—*Corilla erronea, var. erronella.*

this shell (fig. 15), which must now be known as *Corilla charpentieri*, var. *hinidunensis.*

Since dealing with the group of *Corilla erronea*, Colonel Beddome has communicated to me another form, known only by the unique specimen which he received under the manuscript name of *Helix erronella*, Nevill (Ceylon). As manuscript names are a source of great trouble, I am pleased to have the opportunity of studying and figuring this form (figs. 16 *a–d*).   On comparing it with *Corilla erronea*, it is at once noticeable that it has great affinity with that species; it is, in all probability, only a well-marked variety of it, and as it is known only from the single specimen it would certainly be imprudent to accord it higher than varietal rank.   It possesses the same number of plates, but the shell is much smaller and thinner, and the palatal plates are much shorter and placed much nearer the mouth of the shell.   The outer terminations of the parietal plates and the whole of the three upper palatal plates are visible from the aperture (see fig. 16*a*); palatal plate No. 3, which in *Corilla erronea* is nearly horizontal, is here strongly oblique and ascending, while No. 4 reaches nearly to the peristome (see fig. 16*c*).   The form must be known provisionally as *Corilla erronea*, var. *erronella*.

All the known forms of *Corilla* fall naturally into

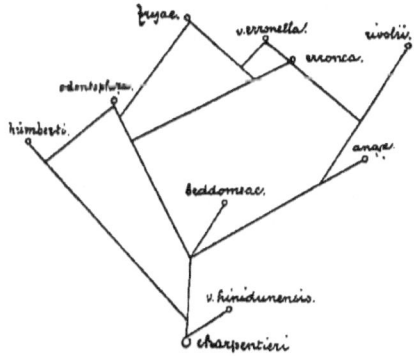

DIAGRAM OF RELATIONSHIP OF CORILLA.

the three groups of *C. charpentieri*, *C. anax* and *C. erronea*, already indicated.   The first group, that of *Corilla charpentieri* (including the var. *hinidunensis*), is without internal plates; the second, that of *Corilla anax* (including the two forms of *C. beddomeae*), has oblique palatal plates; and the third, that of *Corilla erronea* (including the rest of the genus), has horizontal palatal plates.   It will be remembered that the structure of the armature in young shells differs in a remarkable degree from that found in full-grown specimens.   I have pointed out that in the former case the plates are invariably broad and obliquely slanting upwards (see *ante* pp. 90 and 91), while in the latter case they are, in some species at least, narrow and horizontal. From what we know of the retention of ancestral characters in young individuals, as explained by Mr. Darwin ("Origin of Species," sixth edition, p. 388), it may safely be assumed that the immature form of plates found in the young shells

represents the form of plates which were possessed by the progenitors from which the existing armed members of the genus have sprung.   Consequently, those species which have to some extent retained such characters in the adult state (*i.e.* *Corilla anax* and *C. beddomeae*) are the older forms; while those species which diverged most in the adult state (*i.e.* the group of *Corilla erronea*) are of more recent origin.   Assuming that the prototype which gave rise to the armed forms was devoid of armature, the *Corilla charpentieri* group would represent the oldest forms of all, while *Corilla beddomeae* and *C. anax* would come next in the line of descent in one direction; *C. humberti* still later, but in another direction; next *C. odontophora*, *C. erronea* and *C. rivolii* would appear to have branched off in separate directions; and lastly, *C. erronella* and *C. fryae* have diverged from the common stock.   As it is extremely difficult to indicate the true relationship between any given group of species in a linear arrangement, I have attempted to overcome this difficulty in the accompanying diagram.   It will, of course, be understood that this has reference to conchological characters only.

I append a key to the species of *Corilla* which I venture to hope will prove serviceable:

A. Shell without internal folds. .
    a. Shell large, diameter 29 mm.   *charpentieri.*
    b. Shell smaller, diameter 22 mm.
                        v. *hinidunensis.*
B. Shell with internal folds.
    a. Palatal folds oblique.
        α. Two parietal folds   . .   *beddomeae.*
        β. Three parietal folds   . . . . .   *anax.*
    b. Palatal folds horizontal.
        α. One parietal fold   . . . . .   *humberti.*
        β. Two parietal folds .   . *odontophora.*
        γ. Three parietal folds.
           * Shell elliptic, palatal folds short,
              second scarcely curved.
           † Lip much reflected . . . . . *rivolii.*
           †† Lip little reflected.
             1. Third palatal fold,
                almost horizontal. .   *erronea.*
             2. Folds very short, nearer
                aperture, third palatal fold
                very oblique, ascending
                      v. *erronella.*
        ** Shell rounded, palatal
           folds longer, second
           much curved   . . *fryae.*

In concluding the consideration of the genus *Corilla*, I take the opportunity of expressing my grateful thanks to Mr. John Ponsonby, Colonel Beddome and Dr. Brot, for their kind and liberal assistance with specimens and information, and to Lieut.-Colonel Godwin-Austin for valuable information and suggestions.

(To be continued.)

ARMATURE OF HELICOID LANDSHELLS.

BY G. K. GUDE, F.Z.S.

(*Continued from page* 128.)

II. PLECTOPYLIS.

IN the genus *Plectopylis*, now to be considered, we find the armature more complicated than in *Corilla*. In the latter, we have seen the parietal plates to be invariably more or less horizontal, and the palatal plates—normally four in number—to be either horizontal or oblique, and always simple. The species of *Plectopylis*, however, are characterized by the possession of vertical as well as horizontal barriers, which in some cases are double, frequently bifurcate or ramified, and the plates or folds are often very numerous. The genus contains a far greater number of species than *Corilla* (more than fifty being known), and it has a much wider range, being found over the whole of the Indian Peninsula, including the Himalayan Range, Burma, Cambodia, Tongkin, extending north to Central China, with three species in Ceylon, and a reputed single outlier in the Andaman Islands. The Philippine Islands are credited with four species, but the absence of a vertical barrier on the parietal wall renders their position in the genus somewhat doubtful; as the anatomy of the soft parts, however, has not, to my knowledge been studied, it may be advisable for the present to retain these four species in *Plectopylis*. Many of the species are sinistral; dextrosity, however, is the rule.

Plectopylis andersoni (figs. 17a-c), which was described by Mr. W. T. Blanford, in the "Proceedings of the Zoological Society" for 1869, p. 448,

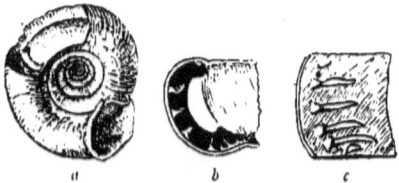

Fig. 17.—*Plectopylis andersoni.*

was found near Bhamo and Ava, in Upper Burma, and on the Yun-nan frontier. It is a solid, disc-shaped shell, measuring 24 to 26 millimetres in diameter, of a light brown colour, with alternating streaks of a lighter shade on the upper surface. It is composed of eight whorls, distinctly ribbed above and below, and very regularly decussated above by raised spiral lines reaching as far as the apex of the shell, the base is also spirally sculptured, but the sculpture is less distinct; the mouth of the shell is unarmed, but the parietal callus forms a raised curved ridge which is

distinctly free at both ends from the peristome. The armature, which is comparatively simple, occurs a little beyond the middle of the last whorl, and consists of a simple strong vertical plate on the parietal wall (see fig. 17a), giving off at its upper extremity a very small horizontal tooth on the posterior side and a short horizontal lamella, 1, 5 millimetres long, on the anterior side, while at its lower extremity there is a slight callus on the posterior side. The vertical parietal plate is shown sideways in fig. 17b, where also the palatal teeth are seen as they appear from the posterior end. Fig. 17c, gives the inside view of the outer wall, exhibiting the palatal armature. The palatal armature consists of four principal horizontal lamellae terminating posteriorly in a triangular conical tooth; above these are: first a minute tooth, and secondly, higher up, a small fold near the suture, while at the base of the palatal wall are also: first a minute tooth, and secondly, nearer the suture, a small fold. The specimen figured is from Mr. Ponsonby's collection.

Plectopylis brachydiscus (figs. 18a-c) was described and figured by Lieut.-Colonel Godwin-Austen, in the "Journal of the Asiatic Society of Bengal," xlviii.

a   b   c

Fig. 18.—*Plectopylis brachydiscus.*

(1879), p. 2, t. 1, f. 1, from specimens found on the high range of Mulé-it, east of Moulmein, Tenasserim. As in that work, however, the palatal armature is not figured, I am glad to be able to supplement the figures there given. The specimen now figured, from Mr. Ponsonby's collection, is old and weatherworn, and it does not possess the marginal fringe of hairs shown in Lieut.-Colonel Godwin-Austen's figure. The shell is described as being of a dull umber brown; it is disk-shaped and regularly coiled, consisting of seven whorls, finely ribbed and spirally striated above; it measures 19 millimetres in diameter. The peristome is strongly reflected and the parietal callus has a strong, raised, flexuous ridge, separated from the peristome, and has, in addition, about the middle, a free lamella, 3 millimetres long (see fig. 18a). The parietal armature consists further of a broad, vertical plate, angulated above, and giving off at its lower end towards the aperture, a horizontal plate, 4 millimetres long, which slopes abruptly towards the parietal wall and gradually loses itself, while on the posterior side there is a very short ridge abruptly sloping obliquely downwards (see figs. 18*a* and *b*); about the middle of the vertical plate a free horizontal plate occurs, about 7 millimetres long, separated from the vertical plate by a distance of 1 millimetre, decreasing in height as it approaches the aperture, and then suddenly terminating (see fig. 18*a*.) The palatal armature is very curious (see fig. 18*c*, which shows it *in situ*), and consists of six folds: the first straight and horizontal; the second also straight and horizontal, but with a small bifurcation at the posterior end; the third partly horizontal and deflecting posteriorly at an obtuse angle; the fourth very short horizontally, descending vertically for a short distance and then deflecting posteriorly; the fifth very short, flexuous, and nearly vertical; while, finally, the sixth is again almost horizontal. A little below, and to the left of the sixth fold, is a small tooth, while above, posteriorly to the first fold, and almost in a line with the bifurcation of the second fold, are three minute teeth.

Plectopylis perarcta (figs. 19*a-c*) was described by Mr. Blanford in the "Journal of the Asiatic Society of Bengal," xxxiv. (1865), part 2, p. 75, and first figured by Dr. L. Pfeiffer in "Novitates Conchologicae," iii. (1867-1869), t. 108, f. 13-15. The

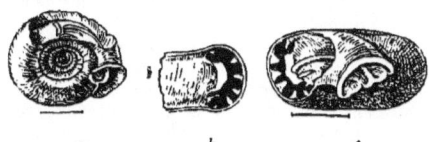

a   *b*   *c*

Fig. 19.—*Plectopylis perarcta.*

armature was figured by Lieut.-Colonel Godwin-Austen in the "Proceedings of the Zoological Society" for 1874, t. 74, f. 4. The species was discovered at Mya Leit Doung, near Ava, Upper Burmah, but the specimen now figured is from Hlindet, and is in the collection of Mr. Ponsonby. The shell is sinistral, disk-shaped, somewhat thin and fragile, and composed of six closely-coiled whorls, ribbed regularly above, smoother below, widely and deeply umbilicated. It measures 10 millimetres in diameter. The parietal armature is composed of a broad vertical plate, angulated above, but gradually decreasing towards the base, where it is also slightly deflected posteriorly. A horizontal lamella rises anteriorly about its middle, very close to it, yet distinctly separate (see fig. 19*a*), proceeding parallel to the whorl, deflecting with it towards the aperture and joining the raised flexuous bilobed ridge of the parietal callus, which

is separate from the peristome (see fig. 19*c*). Another horizontal but very short lamella, below the principal one, also rises close to the vertical plate; a short free horizontal lamella is seen below the vertical plate, but it does not pass beyond it posteriorly (see fig. 19*a*; this third horizontal lamella is also shown sideways in figs. 19*b* and *c*). Lieut.-Colonel Godwin-Austen, in comparing the present species with *Plectopylis pseudophis*, states that the horizontal lamella is not continuous, and it is shown to be interrupted in his figure (Proc. Zool. Soc., 1874, p. 609, t. 74, f. 4), and again, in describing *Plectopylis brachydiscus* (Journ. Asiat. Soc., Bengal, xlviii. (1879), p. 2), he informs us that that species resembles *P. perarcta* in this respect. The specimen here figured, however, has the principal horizontal lamella continuous, a fact which induced me at first to doubt the specific identity of the shell figured by me with *P. perarcta*, but as the second horizontal lamella is joined to the vertical plate in *P. pseudophis* and in my specimen this lamella is quite free, as stated to be the case in *P. perarcta*, it is evident that my shell is not *P. pseudophis*; moreover, Mr. Blanford, in describing the shell, states that from the centre of the curved ridge at the aperture, "a lamella runs up the whorl towards the parietal plication." It may, therefore, safely be assumed that in the type specimen the horizontal lamella is not interrupted, and the question arises whether the shell figured by Lieut.-Colonel Godwin-Austen was perfect in having the horizontal plate interrupted in the manner described. The palatal armature is simple, and consists of four short, somewhat strong horizontal folds, equidistant and parallel, with a smaller one above, close to the suture, and two small ones in a line with each other below, also near the suture (see figs. 19*b* and *c*, the former figure showing the posterior, and the latter the anterior ends of the folds; of the two bottom folds only one is visible in either figure).

Plectopylis shiroiensis (figs. 20*a-d*) is allied to the

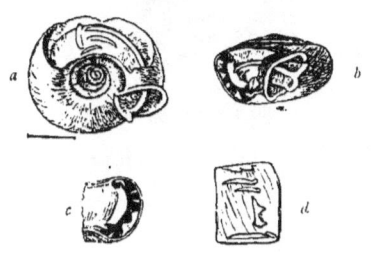

a

b

c

d

Fig. 20.—*Plectopylis shiroiensis.*

preceding species, and is likewise sinistral, but the shell is smaller, measuring 7·5 millimetres in diameter, it is more raised in the spire and the last whorl is less deflected in front; there are also differences in the armature as indicated below. The species was described and figured by Lieut.-Colonel Godwin-Austen in the "Proceedings of the Zoological Society" for 1874, p. 609, t. 73, f. 3, where he states that it occurred in great abundance on the slopes of the peak of Shiroifurar, north-east of Munipur, at an altitude of 8,000 to 9,000 feet, and only in the short grass skirting the edge of the forest. The specimen figured is from the Daffla Hills, and is in the collection of Mr. Ponsonby. The parietal armature is similar in character to that of *P. perareta*, but the principal horizontal plate is more flexuous, being somewhat raised towards the vertical plate and again towards the aperture before its final deflection at its junction with the parietal callus; it is also much broader. The second horizontal plate is also broader and flexuous, while both are a little more distant from the vertical plate (see fig. 20*a*). The vertical plate is smaller than in the species just mentioned, and rounded at the top, while it is not deflected posteriorly below as in that species. There are, besides, two small very short ridges given off from the extremities of the vertical plate on its posterior side; the third horizontal fold is also a little longer as well as more flexuous than in *P. perareta*. The chief difference, however, is in the palatal plates, as may be seen on reference to figs. 20*b–d*. The first is horizontal, small and bilobed, close to the suture, then come two horizontal plates, small but comparatively broad, next a broad and strong vertical bilobed lamella, giving off on the posterior side two short ridges from the

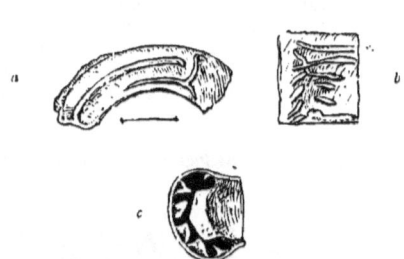

Fig. 21.—*Plectopylis dextrorsa.*

base of the lobes (see fig. 20*d*), and below this a small but broad horizontal plate with a small tooth a little above and posterior to it. Fig. 20*b* shows the barriers from the side of the aperture, and fig. 20*c* from behind.

Plectopylis dextrorsa (figs. 21*a–c*) was originally described by Mr. Benson in "Annals and Magazine of Natural History" (3), v. (1860), p. 246, as a dextral form of *P. leiophis*, from Tenasserim, and it

was figured in Hanley and Theobald's "Conchologia Indica," t. 13, f. 9, and in Tryon's "Manual of Conchology" (2), iii., t. 35, f. 2, as *P. refuga*, var. *dextrorsa*. Lieut.-Colonel Godwin-Austen was the first to point out its specific distinctness from *P. leiophis* (Proc. Zool. Soc., 1875, p. 44), and he raised it to specific rank under the name of *Plectopylis dextrorsa*. He further stated that it is very close to *P. pseudophis*, but his figure of that species (loc. cit., 1874, t. 74, f. 3) does not bear out this view, and, after a careful comparison, I am inclined to consider its nearest ally to be *P. brachydiscus*. The shell, however, is smaller than that of the last-named species, measuring 16 millimetres in diameter, and there are differences of importance in the armature. The parietal vertical plate is rounded at the top, and forms a short ridge posteriorly, while another but much smaller ridge is formed at the base, first proceeding a little horizontally and then deflecting a little towards the suture (see fig. 21*a*); the principal horizontal plate begins at a little distance from the vertical plate as in *P. brachydiscus*, but it is placed above the middle and therefore nearer the suture than in that species, and instead of revolving parallel with the suture it bends upwards a little and proceeds without interruption as far as its junction with the raised ridge of the parietal callus (see fig. 21*a*) at the aperture, while in *P. brachydiscus* it is interrupted. Other differences in the palatal armature will be observed on reference to fig. 21*b*, where the inner side of the shell wall bearing the folds and teeth is shown. The first plate is long and horizontal; the second is also horizontal, and bifurcates as in the other species; next come two series of three folds each, the anterior ones horizontal, the posterior ones smaller and obliquely descending; and lastly we have a strong broad tooth parallel with and near to the suture, with a smaller one posteriorly in a line with it. Fig. 21*c* shows the barriers of this species—parietal and palatal—from the posterior side.

P.S.—With the Editor's permission I take this opportunity of mentioning that as yet I have been unable to obtain specimens of the following species of the genus under consideration : *Plectopylis diptychia*, *P. murata*, *P. oglei*, *P. munipurensis*, *P. feddeni*, *P. biforis*, *P. jugatoria*, *P. revoluta*, *P. phlyaria*, *P. vallata*, *P. eugeni*, *P. lambaceusis* ; and that I should much like to be favoured with them, either on loan or otherwise. In the case of malacologists having duplicate specimens, I should hope to be able to make a suitable exchange, as for instance, *Corilla fryae*, the new species described in the September number of this magazine.— Address : 5, Giesbach Road, Upper Holloway, London, N.

(To be continued.)

ARMATURE OF HELICOID LANDSHELLS.

By G. K. Gude, F.Z.S.

(*Continued from page* 156.)

PLECTOPYLIS ponsonbyi (figs. 22*a-e*), from Hlindet, Burma, was described by Lieut.-Colonel Godwin-Austen in the "Proceedings of the Zoological Society" for 1888, p. 243. My drawing has been prepared from the specimen figured by Mr. Pilsbry in "Manual of Conchology," ix. (1894), t. 40, figs. 9-12. The shell is sinistral, disk-shaped, flattened above, with the apex a little raised, composed of six and a-half whorls, closely and regularly coiled, rounded and gradually increasing; it is regularly and finely ribbed, and has the last whorl deflexed in front; the parietal callus has a raised flexuous ridge, which is separate above and below from the peristome. From the aperture may be discerned a short, free, slightly curved, parietal fold, which follows the deflexion of the last whorl (see fig. 22*a*). The parietal armature

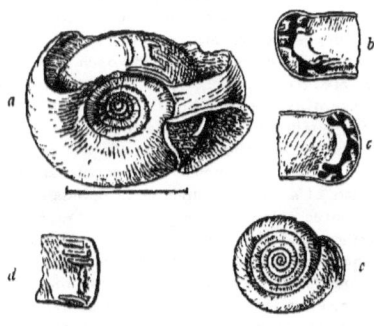

Fig. 22.—*Plectopylis ponsonbyi.*

further consists of two strong vertical plates, the posterior one of which is the longer of the two; it gives off posteriorly at the upper extremity a very short horizontal ridge, and at the lower extremity another short, but stronger, ridge, which descends obliquely; the anterior plate is shorter but much stronger and thicker than the posterior one, and it gives off two strong ridges, one from the upper and one from the lower extremity, gradually decreasing in height. Below these two vertical plates there is a very thin horizontal fold terminating posteriorly a little beyond the posterior vertical plate, and anteriorly becoming attenuated till it is scarcely visible at the parietal ridge, to which, however, it is united. In the figure referred to, I regret to find this horizontal fold is wrongly shown as terminating a little beyond the anterior vertical plate. The palatal armature consists

of: first, a thin horizontal plate, parallel with and near to the suture, a little broader in the middle; secondly, a somewhat stouter plate, slanting a little downwards posteriorly, also a little broader in the middle, and decreasing abruptly anteriorly, but very slowly posteriorly, where it is slightly indented; thirdly, a similar plate, slanting a little more posteriorly, with a slight indentation; fourthly, a stout bilobed vertical plate giving off anteriorly at the upper extremity a very slight ridge and posteriorly from the base of each lobe a short ridge; fifthly, a horizontal fold parallel with and near to the lower suture, raised in the middle, with the apical portion reflexed and angular; it has a very small tooth on the posterior side. Another very small tooth is situate a little below the first horizontal plate about its middle, shown erroneously in fig. 22*d* in a line with it. Fig. 22*b* shows the whole armature from the side of the aperture, fig. 22*c* the same from behind, and fig. 22*d* the inside of the outer wall with the palatal folds (all magnified); while fig. 22*e* shows the shell restored, from above, natural size. The type specimen measures 18 millimetres in diameter, and is in Mr. Ponsonby's collection.

Plectopylis fultoni (figs 23*a* and *b*) was described by Lieut.-Colonel Godwin-Austen in "Annals and Magazine of Natural History" (6), x. (1892), p. 300, where the habitat of Khasi Hills, India, is doubtfully given, but the exact locality is unknown. The species was subsequently figured in Mr. Fulton's advertisements in "Nature" and "The Nautilus," and these figures were incorporated by Mr. Pilsbry in his "Manual of Conchology" (vol. ix., t. 40, ff. 13-15). As, however, the armature has not hitherto been figured, I am pleased to have an opportunity of doing so. The shell is sinistral, subglobosely disk-shaped, widely umbilicated, of a pale ochreous colour, regularly ribbed and decussated by a fine spiral sculpture; it is composed of seven or seven and a-half whorls, very slowly increasing in width, the last of which descends in front; the body whorl bears four rows of coarse hairs revolving horizontally over its whole length, the first on the keel, the second a little below the first, the third midway between the second and fourth, the latter being near the umbilical angulation. The peristome is reflexed and thickened; the parietal callus is only slightly thickened, its margin, however, is distinctly separated from the peristome above and below; the aperture is devoid of armature. The shell measures 18 to 20 millimetres in diameter. The parietal armature consists of a single strong vertical plate (see fig. 23*a*). Lieut.-Colonel Godwin-Austen, in describing the armature (loc. cit.), states that the parietal plate has only a slight horizontal support above on the posterior side; in the two specimens in my possession, however, this plate has a similar support below; these supports consist of a tooth united to the vertical plate by a slight callosity. Below this is a short

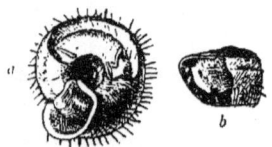

Fig. 23.—*Plectopylis fultoni.*

thin horizontal plate, a little indented in the middle. The palatal armature (see fig. 23*b*) consists of : first, a short horizontal fold, close to and parallel with the suture; secondly, a longer and stouter horizontal flexuous fold; thirdly, another horizontal fold, slightly indented in the middle and deflexed posteriorly at an obtuse angle ; fourthly and fifthly, two series each of two short horizontal folds, the anterior ones slightly oblique, with their lower ends towards the aperture, and the posterior ones deflexed at an obtuse angle posteriorly; and sixthly, near the base, a short slightly bent fold, with the convex side turned towards the lower suture. The specimen figured, which is not quite mature, bears a second vertical plate on the parietal wall (see fig. 23*a*), which appears to be the remnant of the immature barriers formed before the completion of the shell, for, as will be seen later on, in this genus, as in *Corilla* (see *ante* p. 90), the armature is not confined to full-grown shells, but occurs at various periods of their existence, the earlier sets of plates and folds being absorbed after the formation of the next set. A young specimen in my collection, composed of five whorls, possesses the armature a little beyond the place where four and a-half whorls have been completed ; the barriers are almost identical with the mature ones, except that the folds are smaller and the second and third palatal folds are deeply bilobed. A still younger specimen of only four whorls has the armature near the place where three and a-half whorls have been completed. *Plectopylis fultoni* is allied on the one hand to *P. andersoni* (see *ante* p. 154, fig. 17), the parietal armature being almost identical, while the arrangement and structure of the palatal folds connect it on the other hand with *P. plectostoma*, to be considered in a subsequent paper.

The species of *Plectopylis* hitherto dealt with belong to a group forming a section of the

genus, the members of which, with perhaps one exception, do not occur north of the Himalayan range, but are confined to the vast tract to the south of it, comprising India, Burma, and Farther India. Before dealing with the remaining members of this section, exigencies of illustration compel me to consider the Chinese members of the genus, which constitute another section characterized by a glossy, more or less transparent shell and a somewhat less complicated armature. All the known species are dextral.

Plectopylis fimbriosa (figs. 24*a* and *b*), was described and figured by Dr. E. von Martens, in the " Jahrbuch der Deutschen Malakazoologischen Gesellschaft," ii. (1875), p. 128, t. 3, f. 6, from specimens collected in the Province of Kiang-si of China : it has subsequently been found in the Province of Hou-Nan. Dr. O. F. von Möllendorff, in figuring the armature of this species (op. cit. x. (1883), t. 12, f. 11), has given only the anterior aspect of the plates and folds, while my figure (fig. 24*a*) shows the posterior view. The shell is disk-shaped, with the spire a little elevated, subpellucid, corneous, composed of six whorls slowly increasing ; strongly and regularly ribbed above, with a strong spiral sculpture, smoother and shining below, with a yellowish band round the wide open umbilicus ; angulated on the periphery, which is provided with a fringe of coarse lacinia ; the white peristome is strongly reflexed, and a little thickened, and the parietal wall is without a callus ; the shell measures 15 millimetres in diameter. The parietal armature consists of a strong, simple, vertical, lunate plate, the convex side of which is turned towards the aperture, and the lower extremity is somewhat strongly deflexed posteriorly ; on the anterior side are found two short horizontal teeth, one above and one below, in a line with the extremities of the vertical plate, the upper one being the stronger of the two (see fig 24*b*). The palatal armature

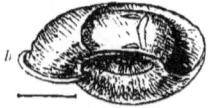

Fig. 24.—*Plectopylis fimbriosa.*

consists of six short, simple, horizontal folds, the first near to and parallel with the suture, the second longer and stouter, nearly opposite the upper extremity of the parietal plate ; the third, fourth, fifth and sixth all parallel, equidistant, and gradually decreasing in length downwards ; a small tooth occurs a little above and posteriorly to the sixth fold ; these folds are visible externally through the shell wall. The three specimens in my collection are from Kioo-Kiang, Province of Kiang-Si, and are all identical in armature. One

specimen is of special interest from possessing, in
addition to the mature plates, the remains, partly
absorbed, of the previous set, consisting of the
basal portion of the parietal plate, the whole of the
first palatal fold, parts of the second and fourth,
and the whole of the fifth and sixth, with the
adjacent tooth. Here we have, therefore, absolute
proof of the absorption of the earlier armature as
suggested in the case of *Corilla.*

The Rev. Vincenz Gredler described a variety of
this species under the name of *P. fimbriosa* var. *azona*
(Jahrb. Deutsch. Malak. Gesells. xiv. (1887), p. 369),
which, subsequently, he raised to specific rank
(" Nachrichtsblatt der Deutschen Malakazoologischen Gessellschaft," xxi. (1889), p. 155). In order
to ascertain whether any difference in the armature
could be detected, I have opened the single specimen in my collection (from Patong, West China),
but with the exception of the tooth near the sixth
palatal fold being absent and the palatal folds
generally being a little shorter, it is identical, and I
am, therefore, of opinion that this form must be
regarded as a variety, as originally suggested by
Mr. Gredler. It is smaller than the type, measuring only 12 millimetres in diameter, a little
darker and less shining, and it is devoid of the
yellowish zone round the umbilicus, so that the
varietal name suggested is very appropriate. Dr.
von Möllendorff has named a variety *nana*, which
differs from the type in having the last whorl with
a more acute peripherial angle and in being much
smaller, the measurement given being 6 millimetres. I do not know this variety, and have, therefore, had no opportunity of studying its armature.

Plectopylis pulvinaris (fig. 25) was described by
Dr. A. A. Gould in the " Proceedings of the Boston
Society of Natural History," vi. (1859), p. 424,
from specimens collected in Hong Kong and in

Fig. 25.— *Plectopylis pulvinaris.*

China, near Canton. It was also collected in
Hong Kong by Dr. von Martens, who figured the
species in " Die Preussische Expedition nach Ost-
Asien," Zoologischer Theil, ii. (1867), t. 14, f. 9,
and this figure has been copied by Mr. G. W.
Tryon in his " Manual of Conchology " (2), iii.
(1887), t. 33, ff. 29-31. It was likewise figured
by Dr. von Möllendorff in the " Jahrbuch der
Deutschen Malakazoologischen Gesellschaft," x.
(1883), t. 12, f. 9, and by Dr. W. Kobelt in Martini
und Chemnitz' " Conchylien Cabinet," ii. (1894), t.
205, ff. 12-14. The shell is disk-shaped, widely perspectively umbilicated, pale corneous brown, composed of six closely regularly coiled whorls, finely
striated above with very minute spiral sculpture
scarcely visible under a strong lens; the spire is

almost flattened, with the apex a little raised; the
last whorl widens toward the aperture and is
a little deflexed in front. The armature consists
of a strong lunate vertical plate on the parietal
wall, strongly deflexed posteriorly, the convex side
towards the aperture, with two short horizontal
teeth on the anterior side, one above and one
below, in a line with the two extremities, the
upper being the stronger of the two. The
palatal wall bears seven horizontal folds; the
first thin, near to and parallel with the suture,
the second, third, fourth, and fifth, larger
and stronger than the first, almost parallel
to each other, equidistant and descending a little
obliquely posteriorly; the sixth smaller and
parallel with the lower suture. There are in
addition, behind the principal folds, two small
teeth, one in a line with the fifth fold and more or
less connected with it, the other midway between
the fifth and sixth folds. The second fold is a
little indented posteriorly so that a separate
denticle is almost formed. The specimen figured
is from Hong Kong, and measures 16 millimetres
in diameter. A specimen in Mr. Ponsonby's
collection is larger, measuring 22 millimetres
in diameter; the shell is darker, thicker, rugosely
striated, and the spiral sculpture is more
decided; the whorls are more tumid and the
peristome is much more reflexed and thickened,
while the margins are connected by a whitish
callus which bears a slight denticle. This
specimen probably belongs to *P. pulvinaris* var.
continentalis, described by Dr. von Möllendorff
(Jahrb. Deutsch. Malak. Gesells. xii. (1885), p.
388), from Canton. The shell figured by Dr.
Kobelt (op. cit.) bears a similar denticle on the
parietal wall. Mr. H. Fulton has obligingly sent
me for examination, ten shells of this species,
the smallest of which measures 16 millimetres,
and the largest 20 millimetres in diameter; of
these, five, including the smallest and the largest,
possess the denticle on the parietal callus, and two
more have a rudimentary denticle.

Plectopylis cutisculpta (figs. 26a-c), from Fud-Shien,
was described by Dr. von Möllendorff, in the
" Jahrbuch der Deutschen Malakazoologischen
Gesellschaft," ix. (1882), p. 184, and figured by
him in the same work, x. (1883), t. 12, f. 12. The
shell is disk-shaped, with the spire a little raised
and composed of six or seven slowly increasing
whorls, finely ribbed above, smooth and shining
below; the last whorl scarcely descends in front,
the umbilicus is wide and open, and the peristome
is a little reflected, the specimen figured measures
7 millimetres in diameter. The parietal armature
consists of a strong vertical plate, a little convex
towards the aperture, with a slight angular callosity
anteriorly at the lower extremity, and with a little
ridge above and below posteriorly; on the posterior

side arc, besides, two minute folds, one horizontal near the upper extremity, the other vertical near the lower extremity, the latter being the larger of

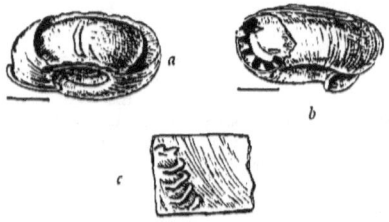

Fig. 26.—*Plectopylis cutisculpta.*

the two (figs. 26a and b). The palatal armature consists of six folds more or less horizontal, the first short and thin, near the suture, the second a little larger, bilobed; the third, fourth, and fifth longer, broader, obliquely descending posteriorly, and each giving off a minute denticle; the sixth very short as seen in fig. 26c. (The first fold has accidently been omitted in this figure.) The specimen is in Mr. Ponsonby's collection.

Plectopylis multispira (figs. 27a–d), from the Province of Hou-Nan, was described by Dr. von Möllendorff in the "Nachrichtsblatt der Deutschen Malakazoologischen Gesellschaft," xv. (1883), p. 101, and figured by him in the "Jahrbuch Deutsch. Malak. Gesells. x. (1883), t. 12, f. 10. The shell is thin, subpellucid, yellowish corneous, shining above and below, widely umbilicated, composed of seven closely and regularly coiled whorls, gradually and slowly increasing, finely striated, the last whorl being wider and shortly deflected in front. It measures from 8 to 11 millimetres in diameter. The parietal armature is composed

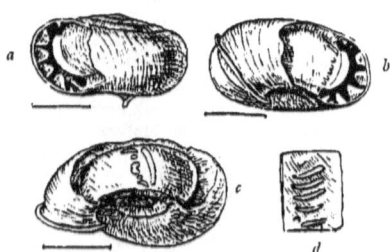

Fig. 27.— *Plectopylis multispira.*

of a strong lunate plate which descends obliquely posteriorly, the convex side being towards the aperture (fig. 27d); on the anterior side are found: first, a short horizontal fold in a line with the upper extremity of the vertical plate; below this, almost in a line, are five minute denticles, the second and third of which are united so as to form

a double one, while the fifth is a little elongated and slants obliquely downwards (see figs. 27b and c). The palatal armature (figs. 27a, b, and d) is composed of six more or less horizontal folds: the first very short and thin, near the suture; the second, third, fourth, and fifth stronger and broader, equidistant and parallel, obliquely slanting downwards, and slightly indented posteriorly; the sixth a little narrower, near the lower suture; between the fifth and sixth folds, a little beyond their posterior extremities, is found a little elongated denticle. Fig. 27a shows the whole armature from the posterior side, fig. 27b from the anterior side, while fig. 27d shows the inner side of the outer wall with its folds. The specimen figured is in my collection, and measures 10 millimetres in diameter.

Plectopylis invia (figs. 28a and b) was described and figured by the Rev. P. Heude, in Part 2 of his "Notes sur les Mollusques Terrestres de la Vallée du Fleuve Bleu," published in the "Memoires concernant l'Histoire Naturelle de l'Empire Chinois" (1885), p. 111, t. 30, f. 4, from specimens collected

Fig. 28.—*Plectopylis invia.*

in Tchen-Keou. The shell somewhat resembles *P. multispira* in outline and texture, but it is more strongly ribbed and less transparent; it is composed of only six whorls and it measures only 8 millimetres in diameter; the umbilicus is very deep. The parietal callus forms a raised ridge, not continuous with the margins of the peristome, and giving off a little above the middle a short entering fold. The parietal armature (see fig. 28a) further consists of a slightly curved vertical plate, giving off anteriorly at the upper extremity a very slight horizontal support. The specimen here figured has, in addition, a second smaller vertical fold posteriorly to the principal one, but whether this is a normal condition I am unable to say, having only a single specimen to examine. The principal vertical plate has also posteriorly a slight support at the lower extremity. The palatal armature consists of five folds, the first, facing the upper extremity of the parietal fold, thin and longer than the others, attenuated anteriorly and nearly horizontal; the second, third, and fourth are short and broad, very oblique, almost vertical, and connected by a slight attenuated callous ridge, which is continued below the fourth fold; the fifth is thin, horizontal, and situate near the lower suture (see fig. 28b). The specimen which I have been allowed to open is in Mr. Ponsonby's collection; it measures 6·5 millimetres in diameter.

(To be continued.)

ARMATURE OF HELICOID LANDSHELLS.

By G. K. GUDE, F.Z.S.

(*Continued from page 181.*)

IN speaking of *Plectopylis fimbriosa*, var. *azona* (*ante* p. 180), I stated that the only difference between its armature and that of the type, appeared to be that the palatal folds were shorter and that the tooth near the sixth fold was absent. Since writing, the Rev. Vincenz Gredler, of Bozen, Austria, who described the variety, has kindly placed two additional specimens at my disposal, and these confirm my statement. The specimens are, however, a little smaller than my own, measuring only 11 millimetres in diameter.

Mr. Gredler has also favoured me with three specimens of *Plectopylis invia*, two of which I opened in order to ascertain whether the second vertical parietal plate already referred to (*ante* p. 181) was constant, and as both specimens possess this plate, it may reasonably be inferred that it is a constant feature. In this connection, however, it is worth mentioning that Lieut.-Colonel Godwin-Austen (Proceedings of the Zoological Society, 1874, p. 609) records the presence of two vertical parietal plates in a specimen of *Plectopylis serica*, a species normally provided with only one vertical parietal plate, and he thinks that to this reduplication of structure is due the more compound forms of armature in the Burmese species of the genus.

The same naturalist draws my attention to the fact that there must be an error in the second locality (Dafla Hills), mentioned by me for *Plectopylis shiroiensis* (*ante* p. 156), as he believes that no European has been in those hills since he collected there, and he did not find the species in question. The shell I figured as from the Dafla Hills is, in Mr. Ponsonby's collection, so labelled, but, as it was collected by Mr. Godwin-Austen, the locality may now, on his authority, be safely altered to Shiroifurar, which is 150 miles from the Dafla Hills, and is the place from which the species was originally described.

Plectopylis stenochila (figs. 29 *a-d*), from Badung, in the Chinese province of Hoo-Pe, was described by Dr. von Möllendorff in the "Nachrichtsblatt der Deutschen Malakazoologischen Gesellschaft," 1885, p. 165, and in the "Jahrbuch" of the same society, xiii. (1886), p. 186. The shell is disk-shaped, with a slightly elevated spire, and is composed of six and a-half or seven whorls, which are closely coiled and increase very slowly and regularly, the last whorl descending a little anteriorly. It is very finely and regularly ribbed and decussated by fine spiral lines both above and below; in addition the periostracum is raised into deciduous plaits, which are especially conspicuous below, and form

a laciniated fringe round the angular periphery. The peristome is white, a little thickened and reflexed, while the parietal callus forms a slightly raised, scarcely flexuous ridge which is separate from both margins of the peristome; the aperture is almost round and is without folds. The parietal armature consists of a somewhat strong vertical lunate plate, its convex side facing the aperture and

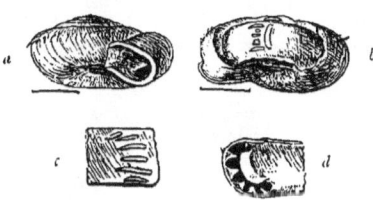

Fig. 29.—*Plectopylis stenochila.*

a little deflexed posteriorly at the lower extremity. On the anterior side there are, besides two short horizontal folds, one above and one below, in a line with the two extremities of the vertical plate, and between these two folds occur four small denticles, the two lower of which are united so as to form a double one (see fig. 29*b*). The palatal armature consists of six folds: the first, short horizontal and near the suture; the second, third, fourth, and fifth larger and stronger, parallel to each other and descending a little obliquely posteriorly; and the sixth again short, horizontal, and near the lower suture (see fig. 29*d*, which shows both armatures from the posterior side, and fig. 29*c*, which shows the inside of the outer wall with its palatal folds). The specimen figured is in Mr. Ponsonby's collection, and measures 8 millimetres in diameter. Mr. Gredler has favoured me with three additional specimens, which differ slightly from the one figured in having only one simple besides the double denticle on the parietal wall. The species is closely allied in its armature to *Plectopylis multispira* (*ante* p. 181, fig. 27), but the shell is smaller, more raised in the spire, and has one whorl less, while it is less shining and translucent than that species. On the other hand it is also allied to *Plectopylis murata*, to be considered in a future article.

Plectopylis laminifera (figs. 30*a-c*), from Hoo-Pe, China, was described by Dr. von Möllendorff, in the "Nachrichtsblatt der Deutschen Malakazoologischen Gesellschaft," 1885, page 164, and figured in the "Jahrbuch" of the same society, xiii.

(1886), t. 6, f. 1. The shell is somewhat solid, disk-shaped, with a conical spire, hornish brown, somewhat coarsely and regularly ribbed, and decussated with spiral lines above and below, but somewhat smoother below, and is widely, deeply umbilicated. It is composed of six and a-half regularly coiled whorls, which widen very slowly; the last whorl descends a little anteriorly, and is angulated at the periphery, which is provided with a coarse laciniated fringe. The peristome is white, a little thickened and reflexed, and the aperture is rounded, without armature, while the parietal callus has a raised flexuous ridge which is almost united to the margins of the peristome. The parietal armature consists of a strong vertical lunate plate, the convex side facing the aperture and only slightly deflexed posteriorly at the lower extremity. On the anterior side are found two short horizontal folds in a line with the two extremities of the vertical plate; midway between these folds is a denticle (see fig. 30*a*, which shows the shell with a part of the outer wall removed, exposing both armatures from the anterior side, and fig. 30*b*, which gives the posterior view, while fig. 30*c* shows the inner wall separately; all the figures are enlarged). The palatal armature consists of a small, short horizontal fold near the suture, and four stouter and larger, nearly horizontal folds, descending a little posteriorly (the second and fifth being a little longer than the third and fourth), and lastly, a short horizontal fold near the lower suture (see figs. 30*a* and *b*). The specimen figured is in Mr. Ponsonby's collection, and measures 14·5 millimetres in diameter. Mr. Gredler has kindly placed at my disposal five specimens, only one of which, however, has the median parietal denticle; two of the specimens measure only 11·5 millimetres in diameter, two others 14 millimetres, and one 13·5 millimetres;

Fig. 30.—*Plectopylis laminifera.*

they also vary a little in the height of the spire, some being more flattened than others. The species is closely allied to *Plectopylis fimbriosa* (see *ante* p. 179, fig. 24); its nearest ally, however, is *P. reserrata*, which we shall have to consider in a future paper.

Several other species of the Chinese group remain to be dealt with, but exigencies of illustration again compel me to break into the continuity of the series, and to revert to the Burmese and Indian species.

Plectopylis serica (figs. 31*a-c*) was described and figured in the "Proceedings of the Zoological Society," 1874, p. 608, t. 73, f. 5, by Lieut.-Colonel Godwin-Austen, who first collected specimens on the peak of Henozdan, Burrail range, Naga Hills. Later he again found it abundant above 5,000 feet on the same range, as far east as the Kopameda ridge. He further states that it is essentially a forest species, found in the dead leaves and moss. The species was also

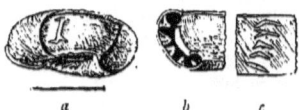

Fig. 31.—*Plectopylis serica.*

figured in Hanley and Theobald's "Conchologia Indica," t. 132, ff. 8 and 9 (1875), but by an error the name was printed *sericata*. The shell is dextral, disk-shaped, with a slightly raised spire, and is composed of seven narrow, closely-coiled whorls. It is of a dark corneous brown above, paler below, with narrow, oblique brown bands, especially conspicuous below, running parallel with the lines of growth. A distinctly angular, raised ridge runs a little above the suture nearly to the apex, the last whorl being bi-angulated at the periphery. It is regularly and finely ribbed, and distinctly decussated by microscopic spiral lines. The last whorl descends but little anteriorly, the peristome is a little thickened and reflexed, the upper part of its outer margin being slightly inflexed; the parietal callus bears a very slightly raised curved ridge, which is united to the margins of the peristome, there being only a slight notch at the lower junction. The parietal armature consists of a single vertical plate, which descends a little obliquely towards the aperture; the upper extremity gives off on both sides a very short support, and at the lower extremity, also on both sides, a stronger support, the anterior one being a little lower than the posterior one (see fig. 31*a*). The palatal armature consists of five more or less oblique horizontal folds; the first is longest, flexuous, and descends a little posteriorly; the second is horizontal, and bifurcates posteriorly, the upper arm straight, the lower descending obliquely; the third, shorter, at first proceeding horizontally, about the middle deflecting obliquely at an angle of about 100 degrees; the fourth is a little longer, ascends a little at first and then deflects posteriorly at an angle of 90 degrees; the fifth is shortest, horizontal, near the lower suture and parallel to it (see fig. 31*b*, which shows the armatures, parietal and palatal, from the posterior side, and fig. 31*c*, which shows the inside of the outer wall, with its palatal folds; all the figures are enlarged). Mr. Godwin-Austen (op. cit., p. 608) mentions six palatal folds, and his figure shows a small one near the upper suture, of which, however, no trace is found in the specimen now figured, which is from Sylhet, and is in Mr. Ponsonby's collection; it measures 11 millimetres in diameter. I have already alluded to the fact that Mr. Godwin-Austen found two vertical parietal plates in one specimen (*ante* p. 204).

Plectopylis pinacis (figs. 32*a-d*), from Sikkim, was described by Mr. Benson in the "Annals and

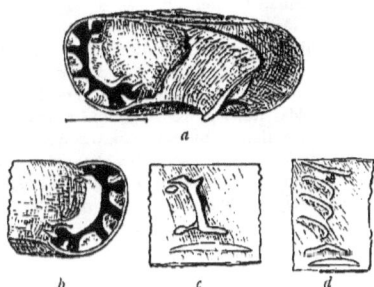

Fig. 32.—*Plectopylis pinacis.*

Magazine of Natural History " (3), iii, 1859, p. 268, and (3), v, 1860, p. 247. The shell was figured in Hanley and Theobald's "Conchologia Indica," t. 13, f. 5 (1870), and t. 84, ff. 1-4 (1872), while the parietal armature was figured by Mr. Godwin-Austen in the "Proceedings of the Zoological Society," 1874, t. 74, f. 1. Professor von Martens described what he thought was a new form, under the name of *Helix (Corilla) pettos,* in the "Malakozoologische Blätter," xv, (1868), p. 158, and this was figured by Dr. Pfeiffer in "Novitates Conchologicae," iii, (1869), t. 101, ff. 7-9; the type specimen, which is in the "Königliche Museum für Naturkunde," Berlin, was obligingly sent to me for inspection by Professor von Martens, with permission to open it; he suspected that it might probably be the same as *Plectopylis pinacis,* and upon opening the shell this proved to be the case, the armature being identical, while no differences could be detected in the shells themselves. Under these circumstances Professor von Martens' name becomes a synonym of the species now under consideration. The shell is sinistral, disk-shaped, pale corneous, widely umbilicated, finely regularly ribbed and decussated by spiral lines, composed of seven slowly increasing whorls, the last comparatively wide and a little deflexed anteriorly, and angulated at the periphery; the peristome is thickened and reflexed, its margins united by the slightly raised, very flexuous, ridge of the parietal callus, which· has a slight notch at the junctions above and below. The parietal

armature (fig. 32*c*), consists of a single strong vertical plate, which is strongly abruptly deflected anteriorly at the lower extremity, and gives off posteriorly a club-shaped support; the upper extremity gives off two slight supports, one on either side, the posterior one horizontal, and the anterior one a little lower, oblique, and very short; a little below the posterior support occurs a small denticle; a free, thin horizontal fold is found below the vertical plate; see also fig. 32*a*, which shows the shell with a portion of the outer wall removed, exposing the parietal and palatal armatures from the anterior side, and fig. 32*b*, which shows the folds from the posterior side. The palatal armature consists of: first, a thin horizontal fold near the suture; secondly, a stronger horizontal fold, deflexed in the middle; thirdly and fourthly, two shorter, but stronger, equal and parallel folds descending obliquely; fifthly a crescent-shaped fold placed obliquely with the concave side facing the aperture (the lower surfaces of these folds are seen in fig. 32*a*, their upper surfaces in fig. 32*b*); sixthly, a smaller horizontal fold, which becomes attenuated posteriorly (see fig. 32*d*); two minute, elongated denticles, one below the other, and placed at right angles to each other, occur between the first and second folds, near their posterior terminations. The specimen figured is from Darjeeling, and is in Mr. Ponsonby's collection; it measures 15 millimetres in diameter. A specimen in my collection, also from Darjeeling, measures 14 millimetres. Mr. Godwin-Austen's figure, quoted supra, shows a short free horizontal fold above the vertical parietal plate; no trace of this fold can be seen in either of the two specimens examined, neither does it occur in the specimen in the Berlin Museum.

Plectopylis nagaensis (figs. 33*a-d*), was described and figured in the "Proceedings of the Zoological

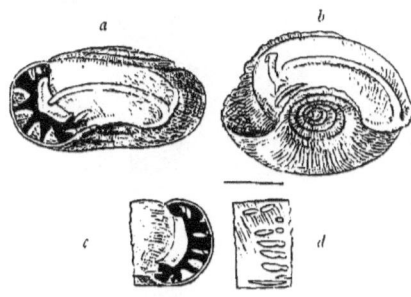

Fig. 33.—*Plectopylis nagaensis.*

Society," 1874, p. 609., t. 73, f. 4, by Mr. Godwin-Austen, who found the species at Prowi, at the head of the Lauier River, Naga Hills, Assam. The shell is sinistral, widely umbilicated, disk-shaped, with a conical, raised spire, of a dark corneous brown, composed of seven closely-coiled, slowly increasing, rounded whorls, the last of which descends a little anteriorly. It is finely striated and decussated by microscopic spiral sculpture, scarcely visibly on the earlier whorls, but more apparent below. The peristome is white, a little thickened and reflexed; the parietal callus has a raised flexuous ridge separated, above and below, from the margins of the peristome. The parietal armature consists of a strong vertical plate, a little deflected posteriorly at the lower extremity, where it terminates in a short strong ridge; it has also a short support a little higher up on the anterior side, and another short ridge on the posterior side at the upper extremity. Below this plate is a free thin horizontal fold, and a little above the middle of the plate, a short distance from it, rises a strong horizontal plate, which runs parallel with the whorl, and descends a little at the aperture, where it is united with the raised ridge of the parietal callus (see figs. 33*a* and *b*, which shows the shell with part of the outer wall removed). The palatal armature consists of: first, a thin bilobed hori-

zontal fold near the suture; secondly, a stronger horizontal fold, with a small denticle at its posterior termination (between these folds, in a line with their posterior terminations, is a minute denticle); thirdly, a horizontal fold, descending a little posteriorly, where it is slightly notched; fourthly, a similar horizontal fold, deflected posteriorly, finally slightly raised and notched; fifthly, a shorter but stronger horizontal fold with the posterior end more strongly deflected and also slightly notched; sixthly, a thinner but longer horizontal fold near the lower suture, attenuated anteriorly (see fig. 33*d*, which shows the inner side of the outer wall with its palatal folds). Between the posterior terminations of the fifth and sixth folds is found a very slight thin fold extending much further posteriorly than the main folds; this may prove not to be constant; it is not mentioned by Mr. Godwin-Austen in his description. The specimen figured is in Mr. Ponsonby's collection, and measures—major diameter, 11·5 millimetres, minor diameter, 10 millimetres, axis, 5·5 millimetres.

(*To be continued.*)

ARMATURE OF HELICOID LANDSHELLS.

BY G. K. GUDE, F.Z.S.

(Continued from page 207.)

PLECTOPYLIS cyclaspis (figs. 34*a-d*), from Tenasserim, Burma, was first described by Mr. Benson, under the name of *Helix catinus*, in the "Annals and Magazine of Natural History" (3). iii. (1859), p. 185, but that name being preoccupied in Helix he changed it to *Helix cyclaspis* (loc. cit., p. 273). Having received additional material, which enabled him to examine the armature, he subsequently published an amended description (loc. cit. (3), v. (1860), p. 245). The shell was first figured in Hanley and Theobald's "Conchologia Indica," t. 13, f. 10 (1870). The anatomy has been figured by Mr. F. Stoliczka in the "Journal of the Asiatic Society of Bengal," xl. (1871), p. 222, t. 15, ff. 4-6, and by Mr. Pilsbry in "Manual of Conchology, ix. (1895), t. 42, ff. 34-36, while the palatal armature has been illustrated by Lieut.-

Fig. 34.—*Plectopylis cyclaspis.*

Colonel Godwin-Austen in the "Proceedings of the Zoological Society," 1874, t. 74, f. 10. The shell is sinistral, depressed-conical, widely umbilicated, irregularly ribbed above, smoother below, hornish brown, with the suture margined ; it is composed of six and a-half or seven slowly increasing whorls, the last not descending in front, and having an acute, compressed keel. The peristome is thickened and reflexed and its margins are united by a raised straight ridge; the parietal callus bears a short, strong horizontal entering fold, entirely visible from the aperture (see fig. 34*a*). The parietal armature consists of a strong and very complicated ramified plate, which ascends obliquely from the side of the aperture near to the suture, where it bifurcates, one arm—the upper one—ascending a little, then proceeding

horizontally, and finally becoming attenuated ; the lower and stronger one descends obliquely at an angle of 45° for about half its length, then deflects almost vertically and gives off posteriorly at its base a short strong support. The lower extremity of the main plate gives off anteriorly also a strong short support. Below the plate is a free, short, horizontal fold. The specimen shown with the outer wall removed in fig. 34*b* is not quite mature, and it possesses the former plate, which is evidently in course of absorption, as the second descending arm has almost disappeared, and the lower free fold is also very slight. The palatal armature consists of five folds : the first, thin, near and almost parallel with the suture ; the second, broad and flexuous, descending obliquely posteriorly, half above and half below the peripherial keel ; the third, also broad and somewhat crescent-shaped ; the fourth, very strong, broad and vertical, and intercalating with the main stem and lower branch of the parietal plate ; the fifth, thin, horizontal and parallel with the lower suture. Fig. 34*c* shows the parietal and palatal armature from the anterior side, while 34*d* shows the inside of the outer wall with its palatal folds. At the base of the vertical palatal fold on the right side—*i.e.* posteriorly—occurs a small denticle, shown erroneously in fig. 34*d*, on the left side. Fig. 34*a* shows a mature specimen, natural size ; the other figures are all magnified. The two specimens are from Moulmain, Burma, and are in the collection of Mr. Ponsonby. The mature specimen measures—major diameter, 17 millimetres ; minor diameter, 14.5 millimetres ; axis, 7 millimetres.

Plectopylis karenorum (figs. 35*a-d*), from Pegu, was described by Mr. W. T. Blanford in the "Journal of the Asiatic Society of Bengal," xxxiv. (1865), part 2, p. 73, and figured by Dr. Pfeiffer in "Novitates Conchologicae," iii. (1869), t. 108, ff. 16-18, and in Hanley and Theobald's "Conchologia Indica," t. 13, f. 6 (1870). The armature was figured by Lieut.-Colonel Godwin Austen in the "Proceedings of the Zoological Society," 1874, t. 74, f. 5. According to Mr. G. Nevill ("Handlist of Mollusca in the Indian Museum, Calcutta" (1878) p. 72), the species has also been found in the Arakan Hills. The shell is sinistral, disk-shaped, with the apex a little raised above the flattened spire, with a wide but shallow umbilicus, white with light chestnut strigations, finely ribbed, with microscopic spiral sculpture. It is composed of six closely-coiled whorls, which increase slowly, the last being a little wider than the preceding, angulated above the periphery and descending anteriorly. The peristome is white, somewhat thin, but reflexed ; the parietal callus has a raised flexuous ridge, separated from the lower margin of the peristome and notched at its junction with the upper margin. The parietal armature consists of a long horizontal fold, united to the ridge at the aperture, and proceeding parallel with the last whorl for a quarter of its length, at which point it

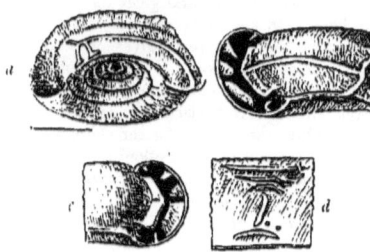

Fig. 35.—*Plectopylis karenorum.*

gives off a shortly descending arm ; it then rises obliquely for a short distance and finally bifurcates, the lower arm of the bifurcation being the longer, and obliquely descending, while the upper arm is slightly curved backwards ; the single arm first mentioned has posteriorly at its lower termination a short obliquely descending ridge, and a little higher up anteriorly a stronger obliquely ascending ridge, while the lower arm of the bifurcation has posteriorly at its lower termination a short obliquely descending ridge. (see fig. 35*a*). Below this complicated plate there is a free, thin horizontal fold close to the lower suture, also united to the ridge at the aperture (see also fig. 35*b*, which shows both armatures from the side of the aperture, and fig. 35*c*, which gives their posterior view). The palatal armature consists of : first, a thin and long horizontal fold parallel with and near the suture ; secondly, another thin but shorter fold which at first proceeds horizontally, then suddenly deflects posteriorly with a slight curve backwards, a small denticle occurring posteriorly in a line with the main horizontal portion ; thirdly, a short, some-what stouter, crescent-shaped fold, with its concave side facing the aperture and lower suture ; fourthly, a strong vertical fold, with two minute denticles posteriorly near its lower end ; and fifthly, a thin horizontal fold, slightly reflexed in the middle (see fig. 35*d*, which shows the inside of the outer wall). The specimen figured is in the collection of Mr. Ponsonby ; it measures 13·5 millimetres in diameter.

In looking over the specimens of *Plectopylis* of

the McAndrew collection in the University Museum of Zoology, Cambridge, I found three specimens labelled *Plectopylis burmani*, Benson, doubtless a misspelling for *P. burmanica*, one of Mr. Benson's MS. names. On comparing them with *Plectopylis karenorum*, I found them to belong to that species. As I have reason to think that *P. karenorum* exists in some collections under the name of *P. burmanica*, and as, moreover, this MS. name was never, to my knowledge, published by Mr. Benson, I have thought it useful to make mention of the above fact.

Plectopylis laomontana (figs. 36*a-c*), from Laos, was described by Dr. Pfeiffer in the " Proceedings of the Zoological Society," 1862, p. 272, and figured by him in " Novitates Conchologicae," ii., t. 57, ff. 7-9 (1863). It was also figured in Mouhot's " Travels in the Central parts of Indo-China (Siam), Cambodia, and Laos," ii. (1864), figs. 9 and 10. As the armature has not hitherto been figured, I am pleased to have had the oppor-tunity of doing so. The shell is solid, disk-shaped, with the apex scarcely raised above the flattened spire, chestnut brown, finely ribbed above, smoother below, with scarcely any trace of spiral sculpture. It is composed of six or six and a-half whorls, the last of which widens rather suddenly, descends abruptly and shortly in front, and is slightly constricted behind the peristome, which is whitish, thickened and reflexed, and has its margins united by the raised, slightly curved ridge of the parietal callus, but a little notch occurs at the junctions above and below. The parietal armature consists of a single strong, solid lunate plate, with its concave side facing the aperture, and deflexed posteriorly below. (See fig. 36*b*, which gives the posterior view of both armatures.) The palatal armature consists of : first, a short horizontal fold near the suture ; secondly, a stouter

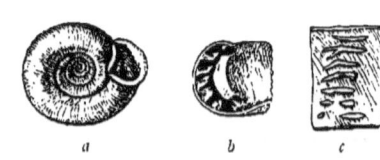

Fig. 36.—*Plectopylis laomontana.*

and somewhat longer horizontal fold, shortly bifurcated posteriorly, the upper arm proceeding horizontally, and the lower and shorter one descending obliquely ; thirdly, a shorter stout fold which proceeds at first nearly horizontally, then deflects a little about the middle, the anterior half being a little indented ; fourthly, a short, stout, straight fold, descending a little obliquely pos-teriorly, and also a little indented in the anterior half ; fifthly, another straight, short, stout fold, also descending a little obliquely posteriorly, strongly indented in the middle : sixthly, two short, stout, slightly oblique folds, the posterior a little higher than the anterior one ; seventhly, a short and thinner horizontal fold near the lower suture, with an elongated tooth a little above (see fig. 36*c*, which shows the inside of the outer wall with its palatal folds). The large form of this species, which is regarded as the type, I have been unable to obtain ; it is said to measure 32 millimetres in diameter, and to show all the palatal folds through the shell-wall. A small variety, stated by Dr. Pfeiffer not to show the palatal folds externally, measures 21 millimetres. The specimen figured, which is from Louang Prabang, Laos, measures 19 millimetres in diameter, and does not show the folds through the shell ; it is in Mr. Ponsonby's collection. A specimen in my collection, however, measuring 21 millimetres, distinctly shows the folds through the shell-wall.

Plectopylis brachyplecta (figs. 37*a-f*), from Moulmain, was described by Mr. Benson in the "Annals and Magazine of Natural History," (3), xi. (1863), p. 319, and figured in Hanley and Theobald's "Conchologia Indica," t. 57, ff. 7 and 10 (1870). The armature was figured by Lieut.-Colonel Godwin-Austen in the "Proceedings of the Zoological Society, 1874, t. 74, f. 8. The shell is disk-shaped, widely umbilicated, dull-reddish chestnut, with

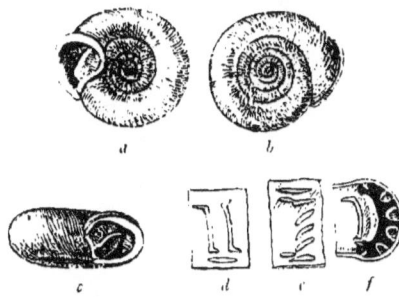

Fig. 37.—*Plectopylis brachyplecta.*

amber-coloured apex, paler below, finely and regularly ribbed, and decussated by minute spiral sculpture. It is composed of six or six and a-half more or less convex whorls, which increase slowly, the last being rounded and subangulated above, near the suture, and shortly and abruptly descending in front. The aperture is ear-shaped, and the peristome brown, strongly thickened and a little reflexed, its slightly converging margins being joined by a thickened curved ridge, which is slightly notched at the junctions above and below. A strong entering flexuous fold is given off from the parietal ridge, revolving over

less than a quarter of a whorl. The parietal armature further consists of two strong, vertical, slightly curved parallel plates ; the anterior one has a short horizontal support posteriorly below, and a strong horizontal ridge anteriorly above ; the posterior one gives off on the posterior side two short supports, one above and one below. A short, free horizontal fold occurs below the vertical plates. Fig. 37*d* shows the parietal wall with its plates and the fold, while fig. 37*f* gives the anterior view of both parietal and palatal armatures. The palatal armature consists of : first, a thin horizontal fold near the suture : next, four short, broad, oblique, nearly parallel folds, whose lower concave sides face the aperture ; finally, a short thin horizontal fold near the lower suture. A little above the second fold and united to its posterior extremity occurs a very short straight fold, while another short, slight oblique fold is found between the posterior ends of the fifth and sixth folds. (See fig. 37*e*, which shows the inside of the outer wall with its palatal folds.) Figs. 37*d-f* are drawn from one of the type specimens from Moulmain in the McAndrew collection of the University Museum of Zoology, Cambridge, the shells having been lent for this purpose by Mr. S. F. Harmer, the Superintendent. It measures—major diameter, 22 millimetres ; minor diameter, 18 millimetres ; axis, 8 millimetres. Among the shells of the genus *Plectopylis* in the British Museum, I found two specimens in the Theobald collection, labelled *Plectopylis clathratula*, Benson, from Balcadua, Ceylon. I am not aware that Mr. Benson ever published this name, but Dr. Pfeiffer described a species belonging to a different section of the genus, from Ceylon, under that name. As no species of the section to which these three shells belong has ever been found in Ceylon, it is probable that there is a mistake in the locality, and it is certain that the name is wrong. Judging from the external resemblances to *Plectopylis brachyplecta*, I suspected that these shells would prove to pertain to that species, and having obtained permission from Mr. Edgar Smith, the Assistant Keeper, to open one of the shells, I was enabled to confirm my suspicion, for the armature proved to be identical with that of *P. brachyplecta.* One of these specimens is shown in three different positions in figs. 37*a-c.* It measures—major diameter, 22 millimetres ; minor diameter, 18·5 millimetres ; axis, 8 millimetres.

(*To be continued.*)

Errata.—Lieut.-Colonel Godwin Austen has kindly drawn my attention to the following errors : p. 205, second column, fifth line from top, for Henozdan, read Hengdan ; eighth line from top, for Kopameda, read Kopanedza. He also states that the locality given for Mr. Ponsonby's specimen of *Plectopylis serica*, Sylhet, is impossible, as these species are very local, and one found on the summit of a range of 5,000 feet and upwards is not likely to occur in a country like Sylhet, only just above the level of the sea.

ARMATURE OF HELICOID LANDSHELLS AND NEW FORMS OF PLECTOPYLIS.

By G. K. GUDE, F.Z.S.

(Continued from page 246.)

PLECTOPYLIS smithiana ([1]) (figs. 38a-d). I also found two specimens in the Theobald collection of the British Museum, labelled *Plectopylis brachyplecta*, which, in spite of some external resemblance to that species, presented sufficient differences to lead one to suspect that they were distinct, and on opening one of them I found that the difference in the armature confirmed this suspicion. In basing a new species upon them, I have much pleasure in dedicating it to Mr. Smith, whose permission to open the shell enabled me to investigate the matter.

Plectopylis smithiana differs from *P. brachyplecta* in being darker and larger. The ribs are coarser and

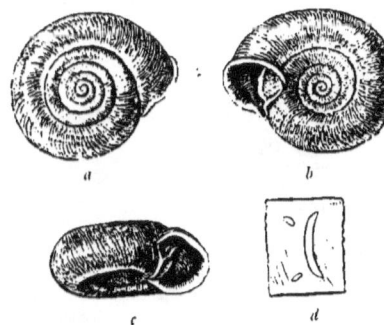

Fig. 38.—*Plectopylis smithiana.*

the whorls more convex; the last whorl is not angulated above, and it widens more towards the aperture. The peristome is less thickened and more reflexed, and the ridge of the parietal callus less stout but more raised, while the umbilicus is wider and much more shallow. The horizontal

([1]) *Plectopylis smithiana*, n. sp. (figs. 38a-d).—Shell dextral, discoid, widely umbilicated, rufous brown, coarsely and regularly ribbed, with scarcely visible microscopic sculpture above, but strongly decussated with spiral lines below, suture impressed. Whorls 6, convex, slowly increasing, the last rapidly widening towards the aperture, not angulated above, shortly descending in front. Aperture sub-triangular; peristome light brown, a little thickened and reflexed, the margins converging; parietal callus with a strongly raised flexuous ridge, separated from both margins of the peristome. Umbilicus very wide but shallow. Parietal wall, with an entering flexuous horizontal fold, united to the ridge at the aperture, and at one-third of the circumference from the aperture upon a crescent-shaped vertical plate, which has two small denticles, one above and one below, on the anterior side. Palatal folds 6, the first and sixth thin and horizontal, the other four short, broad and oblique.—Major diameter, 27 millimetres; minor diameter, 21 millimetres; axis, 10 millimetres.—Habitat, Attaram, Burma.—Type in the British Museum.

parietal fold deflects more at the aperture and there is only one vertical plate (see fig. 38d), which is crescent-shaped, with the convex side towards the aperture; on its anterior side, in place of a second vertical plate as in *P. brachyplecta*, are found two elongated, oblique, converging denticles, one above and one below. The palatal armature is similar to that of *P. brachyplecta*. Fig. 38d, which shows the parietal wall, is from one of the specimens in the British Museum. Figs. 38a-c are drawn from a specimen, labelled Attaram, obligingly lent to me by Miss Linter, of Arragon Close, Twickenham, who informs me that she received it from Mr. Theobald. This was also labelled *P. brachyplecta*, but I have no hesitation in referring it to the new species. It measures—major diameter, 26 millimetres; minor diameter, 21 millimetres; axis, 9 millimetres.

Plectopylis plectostoma (figs. 39a-c) was first described by Mr. Benson in the "Journal of the Asiatic Society of Bengal," v. (1836), p. 351; but from additional material received, which enabled him to examine the armature, he subsequently published an amended description ("Annals and Magazine of Natural History" (3), v. (1860), p. 247). The species appears to be of fairly wide distribution, for, in addition to the original locality, Darjeeling, Mr. G. Nevill (Handlist (1878), p. 71) records the following habitats: Burma— Bassein and Arakan; Assam — Sylhet, Khasia and Naga Hills; while Lieut.-Colonel Godwin-Austen mentions specimens from the Dafla Hills, in Assam. The shell has been figured in Reeve's "Conchologia Iconica," t. 129, f. 782 (1852), in Martini und Chemnitz's "Conchylien Cabinet," 2nd ed. i., t. 64, ff. 19-21 (1853), and in Hanley and Theobald's "Conchologia Indica," t. 13, f. 2 (1870). The armature was figured by Lieut.-Colonel Godwin-Austen in the "Proceedings of the Zoological

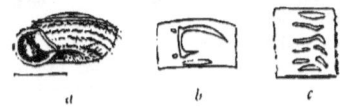

Fig. 39.—*Plectopylis plectostoma.*

Society," 1874, t. 73, f. 2. After looking over a number of shells in various collections, I found that two different forms, one with and one without a horizontal fold given off from the parietal vertical plate, were included under this name, and it became therefore necessary to decide which of the two conformed to Mr. Benson's type, the specimens of which I knew to be in the Museum at Cambridge. Through the kindness of Mr. Harmer I have now been able to examine the type specimens, and I am pleased to have an opportunity of figuring one of them. Although Mr. Benson's reference to the armature in his amended description, "lamina 1 parietali verticali, simplici, lamellis nullis munita," inclined me to believe that the form without the horizontal fold was the true *P. plectostoma*, the examination of Mr. Benson's type shells does not bear out this view. All the shells of the Benson collection labelled "Darjeeling," which are without doubt Mr. Benson's types of this species, belong to the form *with* the horizontal fold, and this form must therefore be taken as the true *P. plectostoma*. Mr. Fulton obligingly sent me twenty-five specimens of each form for inspection, which, in addition to the specimens in my own and other collections, have enabled me to obtain a fairly accurate idea as to the constancy of both forms, the differences of which will be discussed further on. *Plectopylis plectostoma* is sinistral, disk-shaped, more or less dark corneous *brown*, *opaque*, with a conical spire, deeply but somewhat *narrowly* umbilicated; it is composed of seven narrow, closely and regularly coiled whorls, which increase slowly and are a little rounded *above* and *below*; the last whorl scarcely widens near the aperture and shortly descends in front. The shell is radiately plicate and *granulated* by coarse spiral sculpture above, and decussated below, while the cuticle is *thick* and distinctly raised into distant transverse *plaits*. *Five* lines of *scattered* hairs, placed on *raised ridges* pass round the whole length of the body-whorl, the first on the periphery, the second a little below it, the third, fourth, and fifth wider apart, the last being close to the umbilical angulation. The aperture is *broadly* ear-shaped; the peristome is whitish or rufous, thickened and reflexed, the upper margin *widely* arcuate; the raised ridge of the parietal callus is *scarcely* curved, and not perceptibly separated from the margins of the peristome. The parietal armature consists of a strong vertical plate which gives off anteriorly a strong, obliquely ascending support below and a *horizontal fold* above, slightly notched at the junction; on the posterior side of the plate are found two minute denticles, one near the upper and one near the lower extremity. A *single*, very short, free horizontal fold is found below the plate. The palatal armature consists of, first, a thin, short, horizontal fold close to the suture; secondly, a thin but longer and broader fold opposite the upper extremity of the vertical parietal plate, slightly indented in the middle, with the posterior ex-

tremity shortly reflected at an angle of 100°; thirdly, a similar shortly reflected horizontal fold, notched in the middle, and then suddenly deflected vertically; fourthly, a short, thin, broad fold, which has posteriorly to it an almost vertically deflected short broad fold; fifthly, a similar short horizontal fold, which has also posteriorly a short, broad, descending fold, a little more oblique than the previous one; and sixthly, a very short and narrow horizontal fold near the lower suture, situate below the space between the two preceding series. Fig. 39*a* is from one of the type specimens; it measures, major diameter, 9 millimetres; minor diameter, 8 millimetres; axis, 5 millimetres. Two other of these specimens measure 8·5 millimetres, and one 8 millimetres in diameter. Fig. 39*b*, showing the parietal wall with its armature by itself, and fig. 39*c*, showing the inside of the outer wall with its palatal folds, are from a specimen in my collection, from the Khasia Hills; it measures — major diameter, 8·5 millimetres; minor diameter, 7·25 millimetres; axis, 4·5 millimetres. The specimens of this form submitted to me by Mr. Fulton, all from the Khasia Hills, range from 8 to 9 milli-

Fig. 40.—*Plectopylis plectostoma* var. *tricarinata*.

metres in diameter. An immature specimen in my collection has the armature complete, as in the full-grown specimens, but the palatal folds are a little shorter; traces of the previous palatal folds, one quarter of a whorl further back, can distinctly be seen through the shell-wall.

Plectopylis plectostoma var. *tricarinata* (¹) (figs. 40*a* and *b*). A tablet in the McAndrew collection contains five specimens, labelled "*Plectopylis plectostoma*, Bengal, Benson coll.," two of which are distinct from the type and appear to be worthy of a varietal name. Besides being larger and more conical than the type, they are also distinctly keeled at the periphery and have three distinct raised ridges on the upper side, revolving as far as the fourth whorl. I name this form *Plectopylis plectostoma* var. *tricarinata*. The entire shell is shown, enlarged, in fig. 40*a*, while a portion of the last whorl, more enlarged, is shown in fig. 40*b*. The armature is identical with that of the type.

(¹) *Plectopylis plectostoma* var. *tricarinata*, n. var. (figs. 40*a* and *b*), differs from the type in being larger, in having the periphery acutely keeled, and in having three raised ridges between the periphery and the suture, revolving as far as the fourth whorl.—Major diameter, 10 millimetres; minor diameter, 9 millimetres; axis, 6 millimetres.—Habitat, Bengal.—Type in the McAndrew collection of the University Museum of Zoology, Cambridge.

Plectopylis affinis (¹) (figs. 41*a–d*), from the Khasia Hills, has hitherto been confused with *Plectopylis plectostoma,* but it differs in being larger and much paler in colour, in having four instead of five rows of hairs, which are not placed on raised ridges as in

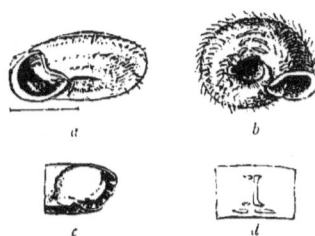

a *b*

c *d*

Fig. 41.—*Plectopylis affinis.*

that species; the cuticle is much thinner and not plaited, while the spiral sculpture is less coarse above and scarcely perceptible below, where the shell is also more shining than in *P. plectostoma.* The shell is translucent and the armature is distinctly visible through its wall, while the aperture is more narrowed laterally and the upper margin of the peristome is less arcuate, being a little inflected. The umbilicus is also wider and scarcely angulated, while the base is much more flattened. The ridge of the parietal callus is more raised and more curved. The parietal armature consists of a vertical plate with a very short support anteriorly at the upper and lower extremities, but without the horizontal fold above as in *P. plectostoma.* The two denticles on the posterior side are larger and more elongated, and below the vertical plate are two short, thin, horizontal folds in a line with each other (see fig. 41*d,* which shows the parietal wall by itself; and fig. 41*c,* which shows both armatures from the

posterior side). The palatal armature is similar to that of *P. plectostoma,* but the posterior portions of the third, fourth and fifth folds, instead of being straight and almost vertical, are crescent-shaped and oblique (see fig. 41*b,* which shows the palatal folds as they appear through the shell-wall); an additional semi-circular fold, posterior to but a little above the fifth fold, occurs in this specimen; this, however, I have not observed in any of the other specimens. Fig. 41*a* shows the entire shell enlarged. My specimens were obtained from Mr. Fulton some years ago; the twenty-five further specimens from the same locality, sent to me for inspection by him, range from 9 to 11 millimetres in diameter. Two immature specimens in my collection are composed of five and a-half whorls; one of these has the immature barriers complete, but the palatal folds are very short and the posterior oblique portions of the fourth and fifth folds are almost straight instead of crescent-shaped; externally a slight trace of previous folds can be discerned; in the other specimen the last immature folds are similar to those of the first specimen, but the remains of a previous set is in a less advanced stage of disintegration.

(*To be continued.*)

(¹) *Plectopylis affinis,* n. sp. (figs. 41*a–d*).—Shell sinistral, somewhat *widely* umbilicated, disk-shaped, *pale yellowish* corneous, *translucent,* radiately plicate, *decussated* by spiral lines above, *smoother* and *shining below.* Whorls 7, narrow, increasing slowly, the last *widening* towards the aperture, and descending a little in front, rounded above, *flattened* below; *four* lines of soft pilose hairs pass round the whole length of the body whorl, the first on the angulated periphery, the second a little below it, the third midway between the second and fourth, which is near the umbilicus. Aperture ear-shaped, elongated *vertically*; peristome white, thickened and reflexed, upper margin a little *depressed*; the raised *flexuous* ridge on the parietal callus is separated from the margins by a slight notch. Umbilicus deep and moderately *wide.* The parietal armature consists of a vertical plate with two short supports anteriorly, one above and one below, and two elongated denticles posteriorly, one above and one below; *two* free, short, horizontal folds in a line occur below the vertical plate. The palatal armature is composed of six folds, the first and sixth short, thin and horizontal, the others longer and broader; the second a little indented in the middle, with the posterior termination raised obliquely; the third is notched in the middle, and deflects obliquely posteriorly; the fourth and fifth are in two series separated by a short space, the anterior portion straight and horizontal, the posterior portion crescent-shaped and obliquely descending.—Major diameter, 10 millimetres; minor diameter, 9 millimetres; axis, 5·5 millimetres.—Habitat, Khasia Hills, Assam.—Type in my collection.

ARMATURE OF HELICOID LANDSHELLS,

WITH A NEW SECTION OF PLECTOPYLIS.

BY G. K. GUDE, F.Z.S.

(Continued from page 276)

BEFORE resuming the consideration of other Burmese and Indian species of Plectopylis, I will deal with a small section of the genus characterized by a thin and transparent shell and a peristome with straight, acute edges. Two species only have hitherto been known, *P. clathratula*, from Ceylon, and *P. retifera*, from India; but a third undescribed form, also from India, has been communicated to me by Colonel Beddome: two species from Ceylon, described and figured by Dr. F. Jousseaume in the "Memoires de la Société Zoologique de France," vii. (1894), pp. 277 and 278, t. 4, ff. 1 and 8, have been referred by him to *Plectopylis*, and, if correctly thus referred, they will doubtless be found to belong to this section, for which I propose the name *Austenia*, in

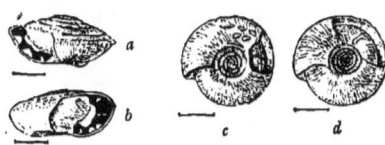

Fig. 42.—*Plectopylis clathratula.*

honour of Lieut.-Colonel Godwin-Austen, who has contributed so largely to our knowledge of the genus.

Plectopylis clathratula (figs. 42a-d), from Ceylon, was described by Dr. Pfeiffer in the "Zeitschrift für Malakozoologie," vii., (1850), p. 67. It was figured in Reeve's "Conchologia Iconica," t. 65, f. 336 (1852), in Martini and Chemnitz's "Conchylien Cabinet," 2nd ed., iii., t. 127, ff. 17-20 (1853), and in Hanley and Theobald's "Conchologia Indica," t. 132, ff. 1-4 (1875). Mr. Benson described what he thought was a new species, under the name of *Helix puteola*, in the "Annals and Magazine of Natural History" (2), xii. (1853), p. 92, but he subsequently pointed out its identity with Dr. Pfeiffer's species (loc. cit. (3), v. (1860), p. 247). It was also figured under Mr. Benson's name by Reeve, op. cit., t. 190, f. 1334 (1854). Mr. G. Nevill (Hand List, p. 70) records *P. clathratula*, as in the Indian Museum, Calcutta, from Balapiat, Sikkim; but I doubt the correctness of the identification of the specimens referred to and think they will probably prove to belong to the new species to be described in the next article as *Plectopylis clathratuloides*.

As the armature of *Plectopylis clathratula* has never been figured, I am pleased to have an opportunity of illustrating it. The shell is somewhat lenticular, widely umbilicated, pale corneous, transparent, showing the palatal armature distinctly through the shell-wall. It is finely and regularly striated by raised ribs, which are more prominent above than below, it is acutely keeled at the periphery, and has two raised spiral ridges revolving near the peripherial keel and ascending as far as the second whorl. It is composed of 5½ slowly increasing whorls, a little convex above, inflated around the wide and deep umbilicus. The base of the shell is shining. The peristome is simple, straight and acute, the left margin being a little reflected over the umbilicus. The parietal armature consists of a single, slightly oblique, vertical plate, which is slightly twisted and a little notched in the middle, and gives off posteriorly above an obliquely ascending support (see fig 42d, which shows the shell with part of the outer wall removed). The palatal armature appears to be somewhat variable, and consists of various denticles, arranged principally in two horizontal series, midway between the periphery and the umbilicus. In the specimen figured, which is in Mr. Ponsonby's collection, the first series consists of: posteriorly, a short, strong, flattened vertical tooth, and anteriorly, two short, slight, horizontal denticles, separated by a short space, the second series consists of: posteriorly, a short, flattened, vertical tooth, a little smaller than the one above it, and, anteriorly, a short, oblique, curved denticle. Below these two series is a longer, but thin, horizontal fold, coincident with the umbilical angulation, while above the vertical tooth of the first series is a minute, horizontal denticle, coincident with the peripherial keel. The specimen measures 5 millimetres in diameter. (Fig. 42a shows both armatures from the posterior side, the anterior palatal denticles being hidden by the posterior teeth; fig. 42b gives the anterior view of both armatures, but the posterior tooth of the first series is here hidden by the parietal plate; fig. 42c shows the palatal folds as they appear from below through the shell-wall; all the figures are enlarged.) Two specimens in my collection— measuring, major diameter 6 millimetres, minor diameter 5·5, axis 3 millimetres—have the anterior portion of the first series, consisting of four horizontal denticles, the first two close together, the third a little smaller and further distant, and the fourth still smaller and still further distant; the anterior portion of the second series possesses, in addition to the oblique curved denticle, a slight, straight, horizontal denticle. Another specimen, also in my collection, measuring 5·5 millimetres in diameter, has three horizontal denticles in the first series, while the second series is similar to that in my other two specimens. It possesses, however, in addition, one posterior and two anterior denticles of a previous set, separated from the mature set by a distance of 1 millimetre.

Plectopylis retifera (figs. 43*a-c*), from South India, was described by Dr. Pfeiffer in the " Proceedings

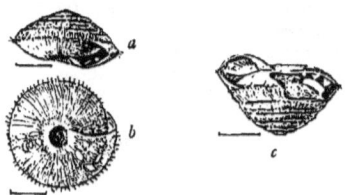

Fig. 43.—*Plectopylis retifera.*

of the Zoological Society," 1845, p. 73, and figured in Reeve's "Conchologia Iconica," t. 173, f. 1170 (1853), and in Hanley and Theobald's "Conchologia Indica," t. 87, ff. 8 and 9 (1872). As the armature has never been figured, I am glad to have an opportunity of doing so. The shell is convexly conical, narrowly umbilicated and acutely keeled; it is dark corneous, translucent, finely and regularly plicated by raised ribs above, finely and closely ribbed below. The periphery has an acute, compressed keel, above which revolve two raised spiral ridges, which can be traced to the embryonal whorl, the lower one being provided with a fringe of coarse hairs. The shell is composed of 6½ slowly increasing convex whorls, while the base is flattened and shining, a little tumid round the umbilicus, which is deep and narrow, suddenly widening at the last whorl. The aperture is subquadrate and elongated; the peristome is simple, acute, scarcely reflected below. The parietal armature consists of a single, strong, vertical plate, slightly sinuate, but not notched, giving off a slight support anteriorly a little below the upper extremity (see fig. 43*b*, which shows both the parietal and palatal armatures from the posterior side). The palatal armature is distinctly visible through the shell-wall, and consists of two series of denticles, the upper series is composed of: posteriorly, a strong, short, vertical, flattened tooth, and, anteriorly, a minute, horizontally elongated denticle, in a line with the base of the posterior tooth; the lower series is composed of:

posteriorly, a smaller, flattened, vertical tooth, and, anteriorly, in a line with its top, a minute, horizontally elongated denticle, and, in a line with its base, a larger denticle, elongated obliquely. Above the periphery occurs, in addition, a small, horizontal denticle, and below the umbilical angulation a short horizontal fold. The two specimens figured are in Mr. Ponsonby's collection, and measure 6 millimetres in diameter. The one shown in fig. 43*c* is not quite mature, the newly-formed palatal armature, near the aperture, consisting of only one horizontal and two vertical denticles. Colonel Beddome has obligingly allowed me to inspect a large series of specimens of this species from the Tinnevelly Hills; of these, nine full-grown specimens possess only one set of denticles; five not quite full-grown specimens possess two sets of denticles each, the older (immature) sets being complete, while the newly-formed sets consist of one, two, or three denticles; four immature specimens have only one set of denticles; ten immature specimens possess two sets of denticles. Of the ten specimens last mentioned, three have the older set complete and the newer set partly formed, five have the older set incomplete (partly absorbed) and the newer set complete, while, finally, the two remaining specimens have both sets complete. It may, therefore, safely be inferred that the older set does not become absorbed until the new set is completed. In a few instances I have observed that the two lower anterior denticles have become fused.

(To be continued.)

ARMATURE OF HELICOID LANDSHELLS,

WITH A NEW SPECIES OF PLECTOPYLIS.

BY G. K. GUDE, F.Z.S.

(*Continued from page* 301.)

PLECTOPYLIS clathratuloides ([1]) (fig. 44*a-d*). Colonel Beddome has kindly lent me for examination a number of shells of *Plectopylis*, from the Anamullay Hills, which appear to be unde-

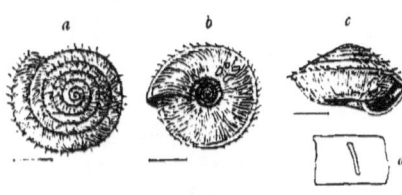

Fig. 44.—*Plectopylis clathratuloides.*

scribed, and for which I adopt the name of *Plectopylis clathratuloides*, suggested by Colonel Beddome. It is possible, however, that this form already exists in some collections under the name of *P. clathratula*; for, as already mentioned in discussing that species, I believe the specimens referred to under that name

([1]) *Plectopylis clathratuloides*, n.sp.—Shell depressed conical, moderately umbilicated, pale corneous, translucent, finely and regularly plicated by raised ribs above, finely and closely ribbed and a little shining below; whorls 5½ slowly increasing, slightly convex, suture impressed. Periphery with an acute compressed keel, above which revolve 2 raised spiral ridges, the lower provided with a fringe of coarse hairs. Aperture subquadrate; peristome simple, a little thickened. Umbilicus deep and moderately wide. Parietal armature, one strong, vertical, simple plate. Palatal armature in two series; upper series with one posterior, vertical, conical tooth and one minute anterior denticle; lower series, with one posterior, vertical tooth and a small anterior denticle; in addition, one elongated horizontal fold below the umbilical angulation and a small fold above the peripherial angulation. Major diameter, 6 millimetres; minor diameter, 5·5 millimetres; axis, 3·5 millimetres.—Habitat, Anamullay Hills, India.— Type in Colonel Beddome's collection.

in Mr. Nevill's Hand List as from Sikkim belong to this new form. *Plectopylis clathratuloides* differs from *P. clathratula* in being more elevated, in having a narrower umbilicus, and in being less shining and more tumid below, while it differs from *P. retifera* in being less elevated and in having a wider umbilicus; it is, in fact, intermediate between those two species. The parietal armature consists of a simple, strong, vertical plate, which is not notched, and is without supports (see fig. 44*d*). The palatal armature is in two series, the first (upper) series consisting of a posterior vertical tooth and a minute anterior denticle; the second (lower) series being composed of a posterior vertical tooth and a small anterior denticle; below the umbilical angulation there is, besides, an elongated horizontal fold, and above the peripherial angulation a small fold (see fig. 44*b*, which shows the base of the shell with the palatal armature visible through the shell-wall). The specimen figured is one of the Anamullay Hills specimens belonging to Colonel Beddome's collection. Six specimens from Madura, India, also in Colonel Beddome's collection, I refer to this new form; four of these are immature and exhibit two sets of armatures, as is the case in immature specimens of *P. retifera.*

Mr. E. R. Sykes and others have drawn my attention to the fact that the name *Austenia*, proposed by me for a section of *Plectopylis* (*ante* p. 300) is preoccupied. Under these circumstances it is necessary to re-name the section, and I therefore propose the name *Sykesia*, in honour of Mr. Sykes, who was the first to point out this fact.

ARMATURE OF HELICOID LANDSHELLS,

WITH A NEW SPECIES OF PLECTOPYLIS.

BY G. K. GUDE, F.Z.S.

(Continued from Vol. iii., page 332.)

PLECTOPYLIS muspratti (¹) (figs. 45a-f). With a number of *Plectopylis* kindly sent to me by Colonel Beddome for inspection, were three shells which he thought would prove to be new. Upon examination I found them to differ from all the described species, and now, therefore, publish this form as a new species under the above name, which was suggested by Colonel Beddome. *Plectopylis muspratti* in outward appearance somewhat resembles *Plectopylis nagaensis* (vol. iii., p. 206, fig. 33), but the armature is quite different. The parietal armature (see figs. 45e and d) consists

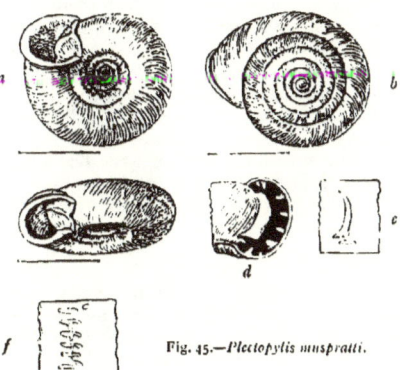

Fig. 45.—*Plectopylis muspratti.*

of a strong, vertical lunate plate, strongly deflected posteriorly below, the convex side towards the

---

(¹) *Plectopylis muspratti*, n. sp. (figs. 45a-f).—Shell sinistral, discoid, widely and deeply umbilicated, pale corneous, streaked transversely with dull brown; finely striated and decussated with spiral lines, which are very distinct on the upper surface, but less so below. Suture impressed, spire a little conical. Whorls six and a half, scarcely convex, slowly increasing, the last widening towards the aperture, slightly angular above, descending suddenly in front, and a little constricted behind the peristome. Aperture roundly lunate, peristome white, thickened and reflexed, margins converging. Parietal callus with a strongly raised flexuous ridge, which is separated from both margins by a little notch. Umbilicus wide and deep. Parietal wall with a short entering flexuous fold united to the ridge at the aperture, becoming attenuated inwardly, and at one-third of the circumference from the aperture, with a strong, crescent-shaped vertical plate, which is suddenly deflected posteriorly at the lower extremity; below this, on the anterior side, occurs a very short, horizontal fold. Palatal folds six, horizontal, short; the first free, with a small denticle posteriorly; the second, third, fourth, and fifth connected with each other by a vertical ridge, which deflects below the fifth fold posteriorly and terminates in a small, oblique denticle; the sixth again free. —Major diameter, 13 millimetres; minor diameter, 11 millimetres; axis, 6 millimetres.—Habitat, Naga Hills, Assam. —Type in Colonel Beddome's collection.

aperture; below, on the anterior side, is a very short horizontal fold; a short, entering, flexuous, horizontal fold occurs at the aperture and is joined to the flexuous raised ridge which unites the two margins of the peristome. The palatal armature consists of: first, a free, short, horizontal fold with a small denticle posteriorly; next, four short, horizontal folds connected by a slight vertical ridge about their middle; the posterior halves of the folds being thinner and slighter than the anterior halves; the vertical ridge is continued below the fifth fold, where it suddenly deflects posteriorly and terminates in a small oblique denticle; below the fifth fold, a little nearer to the aperture, is found a sixth fold, which, like the first, is quite free (see fig. 45f. which shows the inner side of part of the outer wall with its palatal folds, and fig. 45d, which gives the posterior view of the parietal and palatal armatures).

Plectopylis macromphalus (figs. 46a and b) was described and figured by Mr. W. T. Blanford in the "Journal of the Asiatic Society of Bengal," xxxix. (1870), part 2, p. 17, t. 3, f. 14, and in Hanley and Theobald's "Conchologia Indica," t. 83, ff. 8-10. The armature was figured by Lieut.-Colonel Godwin-Austen in the "Proceedings of the Zoological Society," 1874, t. 73, f. 1. The species has been recorded from the Khasia, Dafla and Naga Hills, in Assam. The shell is sinistral, widely umbilicated, light corneous, with incremental curved plicae, decussated by spiral lirae above, somewhat smooth and shining below It is composed of 4½ to 5½ flattened narrow whorls, the last being scarcely wider, subangulate above, a little descending in front. The peristome is whitish, a little thickened and reflexed, slightly

Fig. 46.—*Plectopylis macromphalus.*

flattened on the upper, outer margin; the margins converge a little, and are joined by a thin callus on the parietal wall. The parietal armature (see fig. 46a) consists of a strong vertical plate, which has a minute, slightly elongated, horizontal denticle posteriorly to its lower extremity. The palatal armature is in two series (see fig. 46b, which shows the inside of the outer wall). The anterior series is composed of four short, broad, flattened, straight horizontal folds. The posterior series consists of six narrow horizontal folds, which are shorter than those of the anterior series; the fourth and fifth are a little obliquely depressed posteriorly. The specimen is in Mr. Ponsonby's collection, and measures 6 millimetres in diameter. Two specimens in my collection also measure 6 millimetres in diameter.

Plectopylis minor (figs. 47*a-l*), from Darjeeling, was described by Lieut.-Colonel Godwin-Austen in the "Annals and Magazine of Natural History" (5), iv. (1879), p. 164. As the species has never, to my knowledge, been figured, I have much pleasure in illustrating it. Mr. W. T. Blanford mentioned a var. *minor* of *Plectopylis macromphalus* in the "Journal of the Asiatic Society of Bengal," xxxix. (1870), part 2, p. 18, which is probably the same form. The shell is sinistral, openly umbilicated, discoid, hirsute, finely ribbed, decussated by spiral lirae above, pale corneous with equidistant transverse brown striae; the spire is a little raised, the suture impressed. There are five regularly coiled

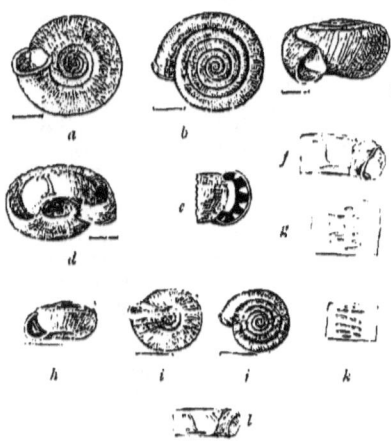

Fig. 47. *Plectopylis minor.*

whorls, the last being sub-angular at the periphery, a little wider than the preceding whorl and a little descending in front. The cuticle is produced into distant, transverse, brownish, raised plaits, which are each provided with four coarse, deciduous hairs, forming four lines which pass round the body whorl. The aperture is lunate, flattened on the upper outer margin, and a little oblique. The peristome is white, a little thickened and reflexed; the margins are connected by a slightly raised ridge on the parietal callus. The umbilicus is moderately deep and wide, but narrower than in *Plectopylis macromphalus*. The parietal armature

consists of a strong vertical plate, a little deflexed below anteriorly, having posteriorly two minute denticles, one above and one below. A very thin, free horizontal fold occurs below the vertical plate, revolving as far as the parietal ridge at the aperture, where it becomes much attenuated (see fig. 47*f.*); this fold appears to be somewhat variable, for in a specimen in Mr. Ponsonby's collection, shown in fig. 47*l*, it is very short, and scarcely extends beyond the vertical plate; while in another specimen, also in Mr. Ponsonby's collection, shown in fig. 47*d*, it is absent altogether. Lieut.-Colonel Godwin-Austen, in his description of the species, states: "Parietal vertical, lamina simple, with no distinct horizontal plica below it."

The palatal armature is in two series, the anterior series consists of four thin horizontal folds, and the posterior series of six horizontal folds, the first of which is very minute, the next four a little broader and shorter than those of the anterior series, the fourth and fifth a little deflexed posteriorly, and the sixth very small and thin (see figs. 47*g*). The specimen shown in figs. 47*a-e* is in Mr. Ponsonby's collection, and measures—major diam., 5 millimetres; minor diam., 4 millimetres; alt. 2·5 millimetres. The one shown in figs. 47*f* and *g* is in my collection, while that shown in figs. 47*h-l* belongs to Mr. Ponsonby, who informs me that it was obtained from Mr. Hungerford, labelled, "*P. plectostoma* from Sikkim." At first I was inclined to refer this specimen to *Plectopylis hanleyi*, but upon further examination it appears to me to pertain to the species now under consideration; the measurements are the same as in the specimen from Darjeeling. An immature specimen in my collection, with four whorls completed, has the armature near the end of the fourth whorl, and identical with that of a mature shell, except that it is smaller. A specimen in Colonel Beddome's collection, from the Naga Hills, labelled with the manuscript name, *Plectopylis minuta*, Bedd., I also refer to this species; it is, however, a little smaller, measuring only 4 millimetres in diameter; it is also a little more raised in the spire, and is more shining and darker.

(To be continued.)

ARMATURE OF HELICOID LANDSHELLS,

WITH A NEW FORM OF PLECTOPYLIS.

BY G. K. GUDE, F.Z.S.

(Continued from page 11.)

PLECTOPYLIS shanensis (figs. 48*a-d*), from Burma, was described by Dr. F. Stoliczka in the "Journal of the Asiatic Society of Bengal," xlii. (1873), p. 170, and figured in Hanley and Theobald's "Conchologia Indica" t. 149, ff. 8 and 9 (1876). Lieut.-Colonel Godwin-Austen described a supposed new species, under the name of *Plectopylis trilamellaris*, in the "Proceedings of the Zoological

Fig. 48.—*Plectopylis shanensis.*

Society," 1875, p. 43, but he subsequently found it to be identical with the present species. ("Journal of the Asiatic Society of Bengal," xlviii. (1879), p. 2.,) Mr. Nevill in his Handlist, p. 71, records specimens from Kuengan, Pegu. As the armature of this shell has never been figured, I am pleased to have an opportunity of now illustrating it. The shell is sinistral, discoid, with the apex a little raised; it is irregularly ribbed above and provided with fine spiral sculpture. There are from 6½ to 7 whorls, which are a little convex above, and rounded below; the last being much widened towards the aperture and abruptly and deeply deflexed. The umbilicus is wide and deep, and the aperture widely lunate. The peristome is white, strongly reflected and thickened, and the margins are united by a strong raised flexuous ridge, notched above and below. The parietal armature consists of a strong horizontal median fold, revolving over nearly half of the outer whorl, and united to the ridge at the aperture, but it is free posteriorly. A short distance beyond it occurs a strong vertical lunate plate, which is deflected posteriorly below, where it gives off a short support; on the anterior side of this vertical plate, also below, a strong horizontal fold is given off, extending a little over half the length of the median fold. A third horizontal thin fold, close to the lower suture, commences just below the vertical plate, and is united to the ridge at the aperture (see fig. 48*d*, which shows the shell with the outer wall removed, and fig. 48*b*, which gives the posterior view of the parietal and palatal armature). All three horizontal folds are visible from the aperture as seen in fig. 48*a*. The palatal armature is in two series: the

anterior series consists of six thin horizontal sub-equal folds, while the posterior series is composed of nine short denticles arranged in a vertical row (see fig. 48*c*, which shows the inside of the outer wall). The specimen figured is in the British Museum, and measures—major diam., 19¾ millimetres; minor diam., 15½ millimetres; axis, 6 millimetres; it is from the Shan States. A specimen in the McAndrew collection in the University Museum of Zoology, Cambridge, labelled *Plectopylis repercussa*, proved on examination to pertain to the species now under consideration. It measures—major diam., 20 millimetres; minor diam., 15 millimetres; axis, 6 millimetres.

Plectopylis stenochila var. *basilia* (¹) (figs. 49*a-c*), from Badung, Province of Hoo-Pé, was sent to me by Professor Oscar Boettger, of Frankfort. It has a more conical spire and the whorls are more flattened than in the type (see *ante* vol. iii., p. 204, f. 29); the periphery is acutely keeled, while in the type it is rounded. The parietal armature differs in having only four simple denticles anteriorly to the vertical plate, the second denticle being very

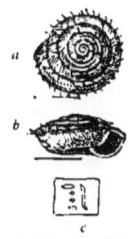

Fig. 49.—*Plectopylis stenochila,* var. *basilia.*

minute (see fig. 49?); the palatal armature is identical with that of the type.

Plectopylis emoriens (figs. 50*a-d*), from the Province of Hou-Nan, China, was described by Mr. Vincenz Gredler in the "Jahrbuch der Deutschen Malakozoologischen Gesellschaft," viii. (1881), p. 15. Mr. Heude, in Part 1 of his "Notes sur les Mollusques Terrestres de la Vallée du Fleuve Bleu," published in the "Memoires concernant l'Histoire Naturelle de l'Empire Chinois" (1882), p. 34, considered this form to be a variety of *Plectopylis fimbriosa.* The two forms, however,

(¹) *Plectopylis stenochila,* var. *basilia,* n. var., differs from the type in the more conical spire, the more flattened whorls and the acutely keeled periphery.—Diam., 6-7 millimetres. Habitat, Badung, Province Hoo-Pé, China.

differ in many respects as indicated below, and I therefore follow Mr. Gredler in regarding *Plecto-pylis emoriens* as a valid species. It appears never to have been illustrated, for the figure given erroneously under this name by Mr. Tryon, "Manual of Conchology," second series, iii. (1887),

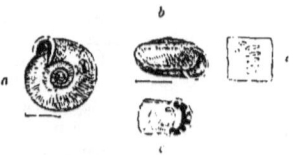

Fig. 50.—*Plectopylis emoriens.*

t. 34, ff. 32-35, copied from Mr. Heude's work, is undoubtedly *Plectopylis fimbriosa*. The differences between the two species are given in tabulated form to facilitate comparison.

Plectopylis emoriens:	*Plectopylis fimbriosa*:
apical whorl *smooth*;	apical whorl *ribbed*;
spiral sculpture only	strong spiral sculpture
perceptible in young	on the upper surface;
specimens; suture *deeply*	suture *not impressed*;
impressed; whorls 4½,	whorls 6, *flattened*; peri-
rounded; periphery *ob-*	phery *acutely keeled*;
tusely angled; fringe of	fringe of *coarse laciniae*,
fine hairs, deciduous;	*persistent*; umbilicus *very*
umbilicus *moderately*	*deep, perspective*; diam.,
deep; diam., 6-7 milli-	13-15 millimetres.
metres.	

The parietal armature is similar to that of *Plectopylis fimbriosa*, but the palatal armature slightly differs, in the folds being much shorter, and the small tooth situated posteriorly to the sixth fold in *P. fimbriosa* is absent in *P. emoriens*, and instead of it there is a minute denticle a little above and posteriorly to the second fold (see fig. 50*d*). The specimen figured is in my collection and measures 7 millimetres in diameter. The palatal folds are visible through the shell wall.

Plectopylis reserata (figs. 51*a-e*), from Tchen-K'eou, China, was described and figured by Mr. Heude in Part 2 of his "Notes sur les Mollusques terrestres de la Vallée du Fleuve Bleu" (1885), p. 112, t. 30, f. 3. The shell is disk-shaped, more or less pellucid with flattened spire, pale corneous, regularly and finely ribbed, decussated with very fine spiral lines above and below, widely and deeply umbilicated. It is composed of 6¼ regularly coiled whorls, which widen slowly; the last whorl descends a little in front and is acutely keeled at the periphery, which is provided with a fringe of laciniae. The peristome is white, a little thickened and reflexed. The aperture is roundly lunate, the margins being united by a raised flexuous ridge on the parietal callus, a little notched above and below at the junctions. The parietal armature consists of a strong vertical lunate plate, strongly deflected posteriorly downwards; on its anterior side are found two slight, short, horizontal folds in a line with the upper and lower extremities of the vertical fold; between these are two, or sometimes three, small denticles, elongated vertically, which in some specimens have coalesced (see fig. 51*d*, which shows part of the parietal wall). The palatal armature consists of a small, thin, horizontal fold near the suture; next four stouter and longer horizontal folds united by a slight vertical callus, and at equal distances from each other; and finally another thin, short, horizontal fold near the lower suture (see fig. 51*e*, which shows the inside of the outer wall). *Plectopylis reserata* is closely allied to *P. laminifera* (see *ante*, vol. iii., p. 205, fig. 30). It differs, however, in being more pellucid and less solid, in the whorls being flatter and in the umbilicus being much more shallow. The parietal armature displays consider-able differences; the vertical plate is much more oblique downwards, and the upper and lower anterior folds are much thinner and shorter, while

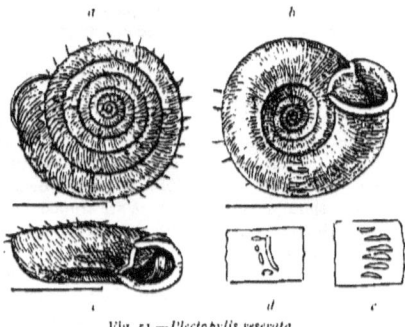

Fig. 51.—*Plectopylis reserata.*

there are two or more denticles elongated vertically between these two folds, whereas in *P. laminifera* there is only one denticle, elongated horizontally, and this is sometimes absent. The specimen figured is from Patong, and is in the collection of Mr. Gredler, Bozen, Austria; it measures—major diam., 13 millimetres; minor diam., 11 5 millimetres; axis, 5'5 millimetres.

(To be continued.)

ARMATURE OF HELICOID LANDSHELLS.

WITH NEW SPECIES OF PLECTOPYLIS.

BY G. K. GUDE, F.Z.S.

(Continued from page 37.)

*P*LECTOPYLIS *magna* (¹) (figs. 52*a*-*f*). With a miscellaneous collection of *Plectopylis*, from Burma, kindly sent to me by Miss

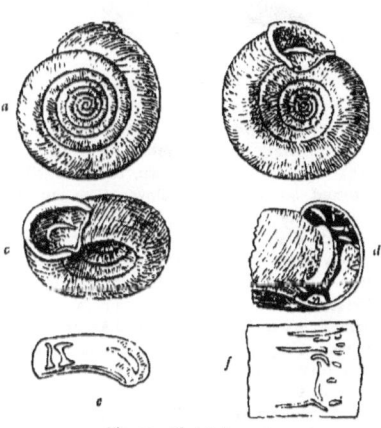

Fig. 52.—*Plectopylis magna.*

Linter, Arragon Close, Twickenham, were two forms which appear to be undescribed, and,

(¹) *Plectopylis magna*, n. sp (figs. 52*a*-*f*).—Shell sinistral, solid, discoid, widely and deeply umbilicated, horny brown, finely and regularly ribbed. Suture slightly impressed, spire depressed, apex scarcely raised. Whorls 7½, a little rounded above, tumid below, increasing very slowly, the last widening a little towards the aperture, descending somewhat slowly in front, and a little constricted behind the peristome. Aperture elliptical, peristome white, thickened and reflexed, margins scarcely converging. Parietal callus with a raised flexuous ridge, separated from both margins of the peristome by a little notch. Umbilicus wide and deep. Parietal wall with a short, entering, flexuous, horizontal fold, which terminates at a distance of two millimetres from the parietal ridge at the aperture, and having at one-third of the circumference from the aperture two strong transverse plates; the posterior one the longest, vertical, and a little flexuous, giving off a short, obliquely raised ridge posteriorly above, and a short, strong, obliquely deflexed ridge posteriorly below; the anterior one oblique, the upper extremity converging towards the posterior plate, where it gives off posteriorly a short, strong ridge, and anteriorly a strong, longer ridge, which becomes attenuated; at the lower extremity it gives off two short, strong ridges, one posteriorly and one anteriorly; below these plates occurs a thin fold, close to the lower suture, revolving as far as the aperture, where it unites with the flexuous ridge. Palatal folds, 5: the three upper horizontal; the first straight and having an elongated denticle below it at about the middle; the second a little deflected posteriorly; the third short, crescent-shaped; the fourth vertical, flexuous; the fifth horizontal, abruptly deflexed anteriorly above and posteriorly below. Posteriorly between the first and fifth folds occur six denticles, placed vertically in a row, the first in a line with the elongated denticle below the first fold. The second a little above and the third a little below the second fold, the fourth in a line with the upper extremity, the fifth near the middle, and the sixth a little below the lower extremity of the vertical fold.—Major diameter, 22·5-25 millimetres; minor diameter, 18·5-21 millimetres; axis, 8 millimetres.—Habitat, Burma.—Type in my collection.

although closely allied to each other and to *Plectopylis ponsonbyi* (*ante* vol. iii., page 178), they present sufficient differences to warrant their being regarded as distinct. Three of the specimens in question belong to the form which I now publish as a new species under the name of *Plectopylis magna*. A shell in the collection of Mr. E. R. Sykes, which had been labelled *P. achatina*, I also refer to this species. This new form differs from *P. ponsonbyi* in being much larger, more solid, and darker in colour, in having one whorl more, in the last whorl descending less abruptly, and in the whorls being more rounded. There are also differences in the armature, *i.e.* the two parietal vertical plates are convergent above, and the posterior one is considerably longer than the anterior one (see fig. 52*e*), while in *Plectopylis ponsonbyi* they are almost equal and parallel; the anterior plate gives off anteriorly below a short, stout ridge, not a distinct fold as in *P. ponsonbyi*, and the thin fold near the suture is distinctly continued to the ridge at the aperture, without becoming attenuated; the two upper palatal horizontal folds are much thinner, the third is short and crescent-shaped, and the vertical fold is not bilobed, while there are several more denticles posteriorly (see fig. 52*f*, which shows the inside of the outer wall). The specimen figured, received from Miss Linter, as above mentioned, is in my collection, and measures 25 millimetres in diameter. A second specimen measures 22·5 millimetres in diameter. The third specimen is not quite mature, the ridge on the parietal callus at the aperture not being formed, but the armature is quite identical with that of the mature shells. Figs 52*a*, *b*, *c* and *e* are natural size, figs. 52*d* and *f* are magnified.

Plectopylis lissochlamys (²) (figs. 53*a*-*f*). The form

(²) *Plectopylis lissochlamys*, n. sp. (figs. 53*a*-*f*).—Shell sinistral, solid, discoid, widely and deeply umbilicated, polished, corneous, finely and regularly ribbed, decussated with minute spiral sculpture above. Suture impressed, apex a little raised. Whorls 7, rounded, increasing slowly, the last twice as wide as the penultimate, widening towards the aperture, but not constricted behind the peristome. Aperture rounded, elliptical; peristome white, rather thin, reflexed, margins a little converging. Parietal callus with a raised flexuous ridge separated from both margins of the peristome by a little notch. Umbilicus wide and deep. Parietal wall with a short, entering, flexuous horizontal fold, which runs close up to the ridge at the aperture, and at one third of the circumference from the mouth there are two rather thin transverse parallel plates, descending obliquely backwards, the posterior one longest and with a short ridge posteriorly both at the upper and the lower extremities; the anterior one with a longer ridge anteriorly at the upper extremity, and two short but stouter ridges at the lower extremity, one anteriorly and one posteriorly; below these plates occurs a thin horizontal fold close to the lower suture, becoming attenuated but distinctly perceptible at the aperture, where it unites with the flexuous ridge.

received with *P. magna*, as above mentioned, I propose to distinguish as *Plectopylis lissochlamys*. Two specimens were sent to me by Miss Linter. Dr. von Möllendorff, the German Consul in Manila, Luzon, however, has obligingly sent me for inspection several specimens of *Plectopylis*, amongst which are two (labelled *Plectopylis refuga*) which I refer to this new species. *Plectopylis lissochlamys* differs from *P. magna* in being much smaller and shining, as well as paler in colour : the shell in shape and texture resembling *Plectopylis pulvinaris*, which, however, is a dextral shell *(ante* vol. iii., page 180, fig. 25). It is more solid and darker in colour than *P. ponsonbyi* and it is more coarsely ribbed ; the two last whorls increase more suddenly, and the last is not constricted behind the peristome as is the case in *P. ponsonbyi*. The two parietal plates (see fig. 53*e*) are much thinner, and the anterior ridges of the anterior plate much shorter and slighter than those of *P. ponsonbyi ;* they are parallel instead of convergent as in *P. magna*. A comparison of the figures will indicate differences in the palatal armature. The specimen figured is in my collection and measures 19 millimetres in diameter. Figs. 53*a-c* are natural size, while figs. 53*d-f* are magnified. Fig. 53*d* shows the parietal and palatal armature from the

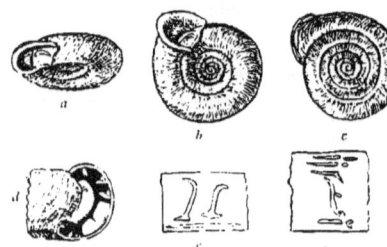

Fig. 53.—*Plectopylis lissochlamys.*

posterior side ; fig. 53*e* a part of the parietal wall with its plates ; and fig. 53*f* the inside of the outer wall with its folds and denticles.

Plectopylis quadrasi (figs. 54*a-e*) was described by Dr. O. F. von Möllendorff. in the " Nachrichtsblatt der Deutschen Malakozoologischen Gesellschaft," xxv., 1893, p. 172. It was collected near the village of Siamsiam, in the Province of Caguayan, Luzon, Philippine Islands. Only three species of *Plectopylis* have hitherto been recorded from the Philippine Islands, viz., the species now under con-

sideration, and *P. trochospira* and *P. polyptychia*, both of which latter will be dealt with in a future paper. As *Plectopylis quadrasi* has never been figured, I

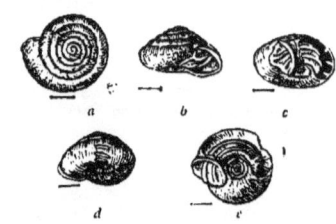

Fig. 54.—*Plectopylis quadrasi.*

have much pleasure in now illustrating it. The shell is dextral, openly umbilicated, depressed conical, thin, dark horny brown, regularly ribbed above and finely striated below. The suture is impressed, and the spire a little elevated. It is composed of six rounded whorls, which increase very slowly and regularly, the last not descending in front, keeled at the periphery, and obtusely angled around the umbilicus, which is deep and moderately wide. The aperture is diagonal, irregularly heart-shaped, and the peristome is brown, a little thickened and well reflexed, the margins being a little convergent and united by a slightly elevated, sinuous ridge. The parietal armature consists of two parallel horizontal folds, which extend over nearly half a whorl, the upper one being the strongest and united to the ridge at the aperture, while the lower one is thinner and dces not reach quite so far ; at their posterior terminations these two folds are united by a slight vertical ridge, which projects a little beyond the upper fold (see fig. 54*e*, which shows the shell with the outer wall removed as far as the peristome). The palatal armature is composed of three short, parallel horizontal folds at one-third of the circumference from the mouth (see fig. 54*c*, which shows the shell with part of the outer wall removed, so as to expose the anterior view of the palatal folds, and fig. 54*d*, which shows the entire shell with the palatal folds as they appear through the shell-wall). The two specimens figured are from Palanan, North Luzon, and are in my collection ; they measure, major diameter, 3·5 millimetres ; minor diameter, 3 millimetres ; axis, 1·75 millimetres. All the figures are enlarged.

(To be continued.)

Palatal folds, 5 ; the three upper horizontal, thin, the first and second with a denticle posteriorly ; the third deflected posteriorly ; the fourth vertical, the upper part deflexed anteriorly, the lower part deflexed posteriorly, with two denticles posteriorly, one about the middle and one near the lower extremity ; the fifth short, horizontal, indented at the middle, with a slight curved denticle posteriorly.—Major diameter, 19-20 millimetres ; minor diameter, 16-17 millimetres ; axis, 6·7 millimetres.—Habitat, Burma.—Type in my collection.

ARMATURE OF HELICOID LANDSHELLS.

By G. K. Gude, F.Z.S.

(Continued from page 71.)

PLECTOPYLIS polyptychia (figs. 55a-d), from Mount Licos, Cebu, Philippine Islands, was described by Dr. von Möllendorff in the "Jahrbuch der Deutschen Malakozoologischen Gesellschaft," xiv. (1887), p. 272. The shell was figured in the same volume (t. 8, f. 8); the armature, however, was not figured, and I have pleasure in illustrating

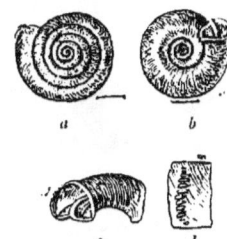

Fig. 55.—*Plectopylis polyptychia*

it. The shell is dextral, discoid, openly umbilicated, finely and regularly ribbed above, finely striated below, and horny-brown in colour. The spire is scarcely raised and the suture is well impressed. There are five and a-half to six convex whorls,

which increase slowly and regularly, the last being angulated above the periphery and scarcely descending in front. The aperture is diagonal, oblique and heart-shaped; the peristome is but little thickened and reflexed, its margins are united by a raised bilobed ridge at the parietal callus. The parietal armature consists of two parallel, horizontal folds revolving over one-third of the body-whorl, the upper strong, and united to the raised ridge at the aperture, which it bisects; the lower thinner, not reaching quite so far at the aperture (see fig. 55c). The palatal armature consists of ten to twelve denticles, arranged vertically in a row, eight of which are larger than the rest, elongated horizontally, and have one or two minute ones both above and below them (see fig. 55d, which shows the inside of the outer wall with its denticles). The shell figured is in Mr. Ponsonby's collection, and measures — major diameter, 4 millimetres; minor diameter, 3·25 millimetres; altitude, 1·25 millimetres.

Plectopylis schistoptychia (figs. 56a-e), from the Chinese province Hoo-Nan, was described and figured by Dr. von Möllendorff in the "Jahrbuch der Deutschen Malakozoologischen Gesellschaft, xiii. (1886), p. 185, t. 6, f. 2. As in the case of the preceding species, the armature has not been illustrated, and I am glad to have an opportunity of giving figures of it. The shell is dextral, finely striated, and distantly ribbed above, finely striated and shining below, light corneous, pellucid, and widely umbilicated. The spire is a little elevated and the suture is distinctly impressed. There are from six to six and a-half convex whorls, which increase very slowly and regularly, the last being carinated above the periphery, rounded below, slowly and shortly descending in front. The aperture is roundly lunate, oblique; the peristome white, a little thickened and reflexed, its margins being connected by a much raised curved plate on the parietal wall,

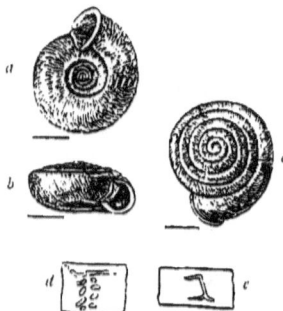

Fig. 56. *Plectopylis schistoptychia.*

slightly notched at the junctions above and below. The parietal armature consists of a strong vertical plate, having a short support posteriorly at the lower extremity, and two similar supports anteriorly, one above and one below (see fig. 56c, which shows the parietal wall with its fold). The palatal armature consists of eight small denticles (above which are a fold and a minute denticle) in two series of four each, the lowest denticle of both series being smaller than the others and nearer together; they are all more or less elongated, those of the posterior series being oblique, except the lowest, which is horizontal, while those of the anterior series are all horizontal; above these denticles occurs the fold just mentioned, which is thin, horizontal, interrupted slightly near its posterior extremity, and becoming attenuated anteriorly, while near its posterior extremity is found the minute denticle (see fig. 56d, which shows the inside of the outer wall with its fold and denticles); these structures are visible through the shell-wall. The specimen figured is in the collection of Professor Boettger, of Frankfort, and measures— major diameter, 6·5 millimetres; minor diameter, 5·5 millimetres; altitude, 30 millimetres. A second specimen measures 6 millimetres in

diameter. Mr Gredler, of Bozen, Austria, has obligingly sent to me for inspection two shells of this species which agree with the specimen here figured, except that one has ten instead of eight denticles, in two series of five each.

Plectopylis biforis (figs. 57a-f), from Ta-kouan-tchen, China, was described and figured by Mr Heude in the second part of his " Notes sur les Mollusques Terrestres de la Vallé du Fleuve Bleu " (1885), p. 111, t. 30, f. 2. As I have been unable to obtain specimens of this shell, I have been obliged to rely upon Mr Heude's description and to copy his figures. The shell is dextral, discoid, plicately striate, brownish, widely umbilicated. The spire is depressed and the apex a little raised. There are six and a-half slowly increasing whorls, which are flattened above and convex below, the last keeled at the periphery, with a laciniated fringe, and shortly and abruptly descending in front. The aperture is semi-circular and the peristome thickened and reflexed, its margins being connected by a raised flexuous ridge which is notched at the junction above and below; about the middle the ridge gives off an entering, flattened fold. The parietal armature consists of two vertical plates united above and below by horizontal folds; below these occurs a short, free, horizontal fold, while another short, horizontal fold is found anteriorly near the upper extremity of the vertical plate (see fig. 57d). The palatal armature is composed of four oblique folds, with a fifth smaller one close to the lower suture (see fig. 57e, which gives the anterior view of both armatures). From the figure it appears that there are besides, four small denticles posteriorly to the palatal folds; but no mention is made of these in

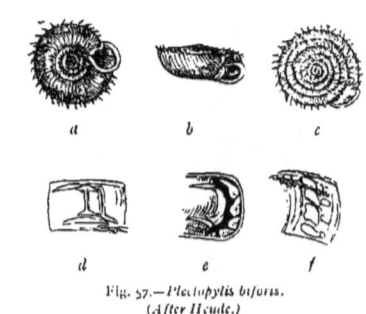

Fig. 57.— *Plectopylis biforis.*
(*After Heude.*)

the diagnosis (see fig. 57f, which shows the palatal folds and denticles as they appear through the shell-wall). The measurements given are as follows —major diameter, 16 millimetres; minor diameter, 14 millimetres; altitude, 7 millimetres.

(*To be continued.*)

ARMATURE OF HELICOID LANDSHELLS.

By G. K. GUDE, F.Z.S.

(Continued from page 103.)

PLECTOPYLIS SCHLUMBERGERI (figs. 58 *a* and *b*), from Halong Bay and Elephant Mountain, Tonkin, was described and figured by Mr. J. Morlet, in the "Journal de Conchyliologie," xxxiv. (1886), pp. 259 and 272, t. 12, f. 2. The shell is dextral, discoid, solid, and widely umbilicated; it is shining, brown, coarsely striated and decussated by spiral lines above, smooth below. The spire is a little raised and there are seven whorls, which are obsoletely keeled above, and subangulated

Fig. 58.—*Plectopylis schlumbergeri.* (*a*, original; *b*, after Morlet.)

below; the last whorl does not descend in front; umbilicus deep, funnel-shaped. The aperture is ear-shaped, and the peristome is white, thickened and reflexed, its margins united by a sinuous raised ridge, which gives off about the middle, a short, entering, obliquely ascending fold. The parietal armature further consists of a vertical plate, with a slight denticle anteriorly near its lower extremity. The palatal armature consists of six small, narrow teeth. I do not possess a specimen of this shell, and as there is only a single specimen of this species in the British Museum, I have not had an opportunity of examining the armature; consequently I have been obliged to rely on the somewhat meagre description of Mr. Morlet, and upon his figure of the armature (op. cit. fig. 2c), which latter I have copied (fig. 58b giving the anterior aspect of the parietal and palatal armatures.) The shell is stated to measure— major diameter, 26 millimetres; minor diameter, 22 millimetres; height, 12 millimetres; but the specimen in the British Museum (fig 58a) measures— major diameter, 19 millimetres; minor diameter 16 millimetres; height, 8·5 millimetres. In addition to the original locality the species has been collected at Nuy-Dong-Nay, Tonkin (Dautzenberg and d'Hamonville, "Journal de Conchyliologie," xxxv. (1887) p. 218).

Plectopylis jovia (figs. 59 *a* and *b*), from Halong, Tonkin, was described by Mr. Jules Mabille in the "Bulletin de la Société Malacologique de France," iv. (1887), p. 99. It was figured by Mr. Pilsbry in his "Manual of Conchology," ix. (1894), t. 40, figs. 1–4, from specimens forming part of the original lot

collected by the Abbé Vathelet. It is allied to *Plectopylis schlumbergeri*, and like that species it is, unfortunately, represented by a single specimen in the British Museum and I have in this case also been unable to examine the armature. Mr. Pilsbry's figure of the structures in question, however, is so good, and his description so minute, that I will copy both.

"Shell depressed, discoidal, very broadly umbilicated, the umbilicus regular, funnel-shaped, its width contained not quite two and a-half times in the diameter of the shell; solid, opaque, obliquely striulate and decussated by sub-obsolete microscopic spiral lines above; reddish under a (deciduous?) yellowish-brown cuticle; lustreless. Spire slightly convex, composed of seven and a-half very slowly increasing whorls; the last whorl wider, *rather strongly deflexed in front*, very convex beneath, and obtusely subangulated around the umbilicus. Aperture oblique, rotund-truncate, the peristome well curved, strongly reflexed, its face white and thickened, ends joined by an *elevated lobe of the parietal callus*, from which an entering lamella arises extending a short distance inward. At the last third within the whorl it is obstructed by a broad, curved, transverse parietal plate, the convexity of the curve outward, *the upper border of it slightly scalloped*; a minute denticle stands in front of the lower end of this plate. The outer wall bears seven plicae: the two outer small, parallel to the sutures; the next to the lowest fold

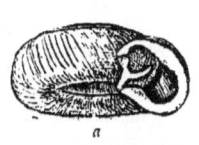 

Fig. 59.—*Plectopylis jovia.* (*a*, original; *b*, after Pilsbry.)

very minute, situated somewhat back of the others; the four median larger and directed obliquely across the whorl. Altitude, 13 millimetres; diameter, 29–31 millimetres. It is not improbable that both *jovia* and *villedaryi* will prove to be varietal forms of *schlumbergeri*" (Pilsbry, "Manual of Conchology," viii. (1893), p. 156).

Fig. 59b, enlarged, is copied from "Manual of Conchology," ix. (1894), t. 40, f. 4. The specimen shown in fig. 59a is in the British Museum, and measures—major diameter, 30 millimetres ; minor diameter, 26 millimetres ; altitude, 15 millimetres.

Plectopylis villedaryi (figs. 60 *a* and *b*), from Langson and Bac-ninh, Tonkin, was described and figured by Mr. C. F. Ancey in " Le Naturaliste," 1888, p. 71, f. 2. Mr. Pilsbry has illustrated the armature in " Manual of Conchology," viii. (1893), t. 43, f. 39, which I have been obliged to copy, having only seen one unbroken specimen of this species. The shell is solid, depressed, disk-shaped, regularly ribbed with minute spiral sculpture above, the ribs being particularly conspicuous in the wide funnel-shaped umbilicus. There are six and a-half whorls, which increase slowly and regularly, the last descending in front, very convex and subangular around the umbilicus. The aperture is very oblique, somewhat ear-shaped, and the peristome is very much thickened and reflexed, the margins being united by an elevated tongue-shaped ridge on the parietal

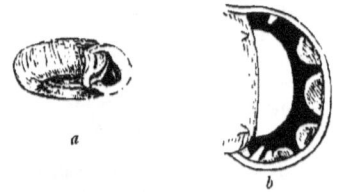

Fig. 60.—*Plectopylis villedaryi.* (*a*, original *b*, after Pilsbry.)

callus. A stout curved plate is given off from this ridge, rising obliquely (see fig. 60*a*). The parietal armature is composed of a strong vertical plate with two denticles anteriorly, one near the upper and one near the lower extremity, the upper one smaller, the lower one elongated (see fig. 60*b*, which gives the anterior view of both armatures). The palatal armature consists of seven folds, the first small and thin, near to and parallel with the upper suture ; the second, third, fourth and fifth larger, oblique ; the sixth very minute and situated to the rear of the others ; the seventh small, near to and parallel with the lower suture (see fig. 60*b*). The measurements given are : major diameter, 20 millimetres ; minor diameter, 17 millimetres ; altitude, 9 millimetres. The shell in the British Museum (shown in fig. 60*a*) measures—major diameter, 19 millimetres ; minor diameter, 16½ millimetres ; altitude, 8 millimetres.

Plectopylis phlyaria (figs. 61*a*-*c*), from Tonkin, was described and figured, by Mr. Mabille, in " Bulletin de la Société Malacologique de France," iv. (1887), p. 100, t. 2, ff. 1-3. Unfortunately the armature does not appear to have been examined by Mr. Mabille, for not only has he omitted to illustrate it, but no mention is made of it in his diagnoses, and to my great regret these important structures

remain unknown to me. Not having been able to obtain a specimen of this species I have been under the necessity of copying Mr. Mabille's figures and description. The shell is "openly umbilicated, depressed discoid, thin, somewhat solid, scarcely

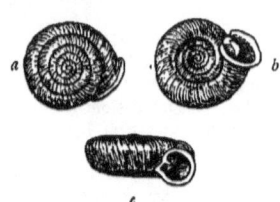

Fig. 61.—*Plectopylis phlyaria.* (After Mabille.

shining, dull whitish under a deciduous, greyish, hairy cuticle, arcuately striated, and seen under a lens to be covered with imbricating lamellae. Spire flat, apex shining, smooth, corneous. Whorls seven and a-half, narrow, convex, rather rapidly and regularly increasing, separated by a deeply impressed suture. The last whorl large, but little wider than the preceding whorl if viewed from above ; laterally compressed, obscurely angulated at the periphery, deeply descending in front, tortuous, a little convex beneath. Aperture half round, toothed, the margins connected by a transverse parietal lamina, behind which a dentiform callus emerges ; peristome white, thick, reflexed. Major diameter, 15 millimetres, minor diameter, 13 millimetres ; altitude, 5·5 millimetres."

(To be continued.)

ARMATURE OF HELICOID LANDSHELLS.

By G. K. Gude, F.Z.S.

(Continued from page 139.)

PLECTOPYLIS pseudophis (figs. 62a-c) from Thyet-myo, Pegu, was described and figured by Lieut.-Colonel Godwin-Austen, in the "Proceedings of the Zoological Society," 1874, p. 610, t. 74, figs. 3 and 3a. The shell is sinistral, disk-shaped, pale horny in colour, and widely umbilicated The spire is a little elevated, and the suture slightly impressed. There are seven whorls, which increase slowly and

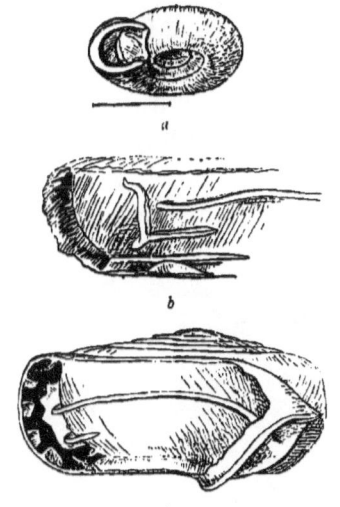

regularly; the last whorl is subangulated above, rounded below, and descends rather deeply and suddenly in front. The aperture is rounded, and the peristome is thickened and reflected, the margins being connected by a raised flexuous ridge on the parietal callus, slightly notched at the junctions above and below. The parietal armature consists of a strong vertical plate, deflected posteriorly at the upper extremity, and giving off at the lower extremity an obliquely descending ridge posteriorly and a short horizontal fold anteriorly; the vertical plate is toothed in outline in the upper half, the teeth intercalating with three of the palatal folds (see fig. 62c). A long horizontal fold rises close to the vertical plate anteriorly, revolving as far as the aperture, where it unites with the raised flexuous ridge; a thin slight fold runs near to and parallel with the

lower suture (see figs. 62b and c, which shows the shell with part of the outer wall removed). The palatal armature consists of six simple short folds, the lowest three the longest and highest, the sixth much arched outwards (see fig. 62c). To my regret I have been unable to examine the armature of this species, having seen but a single specimen, which is in the British Museum; this is shown in fig. 62a; it measures—major diameter, 12 milli-metres; minor diameter, 10 millimetres; altitude, 5 millimetres. Figs. 62b and c are copied from "Proceedings of the Zoological Society," 1874, t. 74, figs. 3 and 3a.

Plectopylis brahma (figs. 63a-c), from Brahmakhund, Eastern Assam, was described and figured by Lieut.-Colonel Godwin-Austen in the "Journal of the Asiatic Society of Bengal," xlviii. (1879), p. 3, t. 1, f. 3. The shell is sinistral, disk-shaped, pale horny-brown, finely and regularly striated, with a moderately wide umbilicus. The spire is slightly raised, and the apex is a little elevated. There are seven whorls, which are slightly convex, and increase slowly and regularly; the last is angular above, rounded below, a little constricted behind the peristome, and scarcely descending in front. The aperture is obliquely lunate, and the peristome is white, a little thickened and reflexed, the margins being connected by a scarcely raised curved ridge on the parietal callus; the ridge is notched at the junctions above and below. The parietal armature consists of a strong vertical plate having a short support posteriorly above and below, and giving off anteriorly at the lower extremity a short horizontal fold; above this are two free longer horizontal folds, the upper one rising close to the vertical plate, the lower one longer

Fig. 63.—*Plectopylis brahma.*

and rising a little further from the vertical fold. A minute denticle occurs between the second and third horizontal folds, and a horizontally elongated denticle above the upper extremity of the vertical fold; a very thin slight fold runs near to and parallel with the lower suture, uniting with the ridge at the aperture (see fig. 63c, which shows the

Fig. 62.—*Plectopylis pseudophis.* (*a*, original; *b* and *c*, after Godwin-Austen.)

parietal wall with its folds). The palatal armature is in two series, the anterior one consisting of
four elongated horizontal folds, the second and
third being separated by a wider space than the
others, while the posterior series is composed of
thirteen or fourteen minute denticles arranged
close together, some a little elongated. The shell
figured is in the British Museum. It measures—
major diameter, 8 millimetres; minor diameter,
6·5 millimetres; altitude, 4·5 millimetres.

Plectopylis feddeni (figs. 64a-d), from Prome, in
the Pegu district of Burma, was described by Mr.
W. T. Blanford in the "Journal of the Asiatic
Society of Bengal," xxx. (1865), p. 75. The shell
was figured in Hanley and Theobald's "Conchologia Indica" (1875), t. 131, ff. 1-3, while
Lieut.-Colonel Godwin-Austen has illustrated the
parietal armature ("Proceedings Zoological Society" (1874), t. 74, f. 7), and as I have been unable
to obtain a specimen, I have copied these figures.
According to Mr. Neville's Hand List, p. 71, the
Calcutta Museum possesses specimens from Thyet-

the anterior side of the first vertical fold, is found
a small denticle. Above and below there is a
similar free horizontal fold (see fig. 64d). The
palatal armature consists of five folds, which are
at first horizontal but become vertical posteriorly;
the first and second are longer than the rest. The
measurements are stated to be—major diameter,
16 millimetres; minor diameter, 13 millimetres;
altitude, 4·5 millimetres.

(To be continued.)

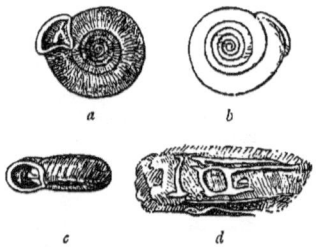

Fig. 64.—*Plectopylis feddeni.* (a-c, after Hanley and
Theobald; d, after Godwin-Austen.)

myo. The description and figures referred to
show that the shell is sinistral, discoid, very
widely umbilicated, thin, whitish, irregularly and
obliquely sculptured; the spire is plane and the
suture impressed. There are six and a-half to
seven narrow whorls, which increase slowly and
regularly, and are a little convex above; the last
is much wider, rounded at the periphery and base,
and abruptly descends in front. The peristome
is a little thickened and reflexed, and the margins
are united by a raised flexuous ridge. From
the middle of the ridge a horizontal, entering,
interrupted fold is given off. The parietal armature consists of three vertical folds, of which
the posterior one is longest and free, and gives off
posteriorly at its lower extremity a short ridge;
the two anterior ones are equal in length and are
united by two horizontal folds, of which the upper
one continues anteriorly to the ridge at the aperture, while the lower one is very short and projects
only a little way beyond the first vertical fold;
between these two horizontal folds, and close to

ARMATURE OF HELICOID LANDSHELLS

WITH NEW SPECIES OF PLECTOPYLIS.

BY G. K. GUDE, F.Z.S.

(Continued from page 171.)

*P*LECTOPYLIS *secura* (figs. 65*a-d*), from Si-lin, in the Chinese province Kouang-Si, was described by Mr. Heude in the "Journal de Conchyliologie," xxxvii. (1889), p. 226, and figured in the third part of his "Notes sur les Mollusques terrestres de la Vallée du Fleuve bleu" (1890), t. 38, f. 6. Not having been able to obtain a specimen of this shell, I have been obliged to rely upon Mr. Heude's description and to copy his figures. The shell is described as dextral, discoid, greenish horn-coloured, striated above, shining below, and widely umbilicated, with the spire flattened and the apex scarcely raised. There are six rounded whorls, which increase regularly, the last scarcely descending in front; the aperture is semi-lunate and strongly oblique; the peristome narrow and reflexed; the margins are united by a raised flexuous ridge on the parietal wall, and there is an entering horizontal fold. The parietal armature consists of a single vertical plate, which appears to be a little deflected anteriorly below (see fig. 65*d*). The palatal armature, as figured, appears to consist of six oblique folds, although the author only mentions four in his diagnosis; the first fold is minute, situate near the upper suture, the next four stout and oblique, and the sixth thinner and apparently horizontal (see fig 65*d*). The measurements given are—major diameter,

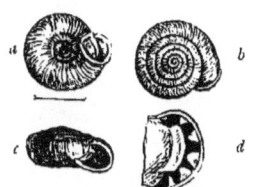

Fig. 65.—*Plectopylis secura* (after Heude).

9 millimetres; minor diameter, 7 millimetres; altitude, 4 millimetres.

Plectopylis leucochilus [1] (figs. 66*a-e*). Five shells, labelled "Burma," without further indication of

[1] *Plectopylis leucochilus*, n. sp. (figs. 66*a-e*). — Shell sinistral, rather solid, discoid, deeply and perspectively umbilicated, pale yellowish-corneous finely and regularly ribbed, ornamented with minute spiral sculpture. Suture almost linear, spire depressed, apex scarcely raised. Whorls seven to seven and a-half, a little rounded above, rather tumid below, increasing slowly and regularly, the last descending abruptly and rather deeply in front. Aperture roundly oval; peristome white, a little thickened and strongly reflexed, the margins a little converging; parietal callus with a slightly raised flexuous ridge, separated from both margins of the peristome by a little notch. Umbilicus deep, widely perspective. Parietal wall

locality, received by the writer, from Mr. Hugh Fulton, under the name of *Plectopylis leiophis*, proved upon examination to be distinct, and to belong, in fact, to a different group of *Plectopylis*. They represent a species—for which I propose the name

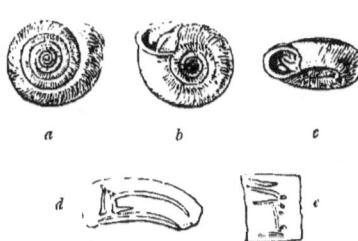

Fig. 66.—*Plectopylis leucochilus.*

Plectopylis leucochilus—allied to *P. ponsonbyi*, but differing from it in the more raised spire and in having a deeper and more perspective umbilicus. In the armature this new species differs from the other members of the group of *P. ponsonbyi* in having the upper parietal fold uninterrupted. Figs. 66*a-c* show the shell in three different aspects, natural size, while figs. 66*d* and *e* are enlarged; the former shows the parietal wall with its plates and folds, and the latter the inside of the outer wall with the folds and denticles.

Plectopylis perrierae [2] (figs. 67*a-f*).—Two specimens of an undescribed *Plectopylis* have been

with two transverse oblique plates converging upwards, the posterior one rather thin, slightly sinuous, and having a short ridge posteriorly at the upper and lower extremities, the anterior one shorter, but much stronger and stouter, having an ascending ridge posteriorly above and a short stout support posteriorly below; on the anterior side are found two strong horizontal folds, the lower stout and short and becoming suddenly attenuated; the upper fold long, rather thinner, following the deflection of the last whorl and terminating close to the ridge at the aperture, but not being united to it; a very thin horizontal fold rises below the transverse plates close to the lower suture, runs parallel with it, and terminates at the ridge at the aperture. Palatal folds, five: the first near the suture, straight and nearly horizontal; the second a little more oblique and deflected posteriorly; the third nearly horizontal, but more deflected posteriorly; all three have a slight indentation near the posterior extremity forming a bead-like termination; the fourth is vertical, deflected a little anteriorly above and posteriorly below, having posteriorly a small denticle near the lower extremity and another about the middle; the fifth is near the lower suture, horizontal and deflected at both extremities.—Major diameter, 15-17 millimetres; minor diameter, 12-14 millimetres; altitude, 6-7 millimetres.—Habitat, Burma.—Type in my collection.

[2] *Plectopylis perrierae*, n. sp. (figs. 67*a-f*). Shell sinistral, discoid, widely and deeply umbilicated, pale corneous, very finely and regularly striated, and decussated by spiral lines. Suture slightly impressed, spire flattened, apex a little raised, whorls six to seven, increasing slowly and regularly, flattened above, rounded below, the last angulated above the periphery

obligingly placed in my hands by Miss Linter, at whose request 1 name it after her friend, Mrs.

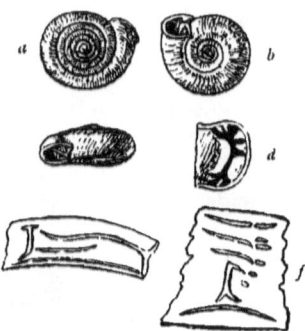

Fig. 67.—*Plectopylis perrierae.*

parietal and palatal armatures from the posterior side; *e*, the inside of the outer wall with the palatal folds and denticles; and *f*, the parietal wall with its plate and folds.

(To be continued.)

Lumley Perrier. In contour this new species resembles *Plectopylis perarcta (ante* vol. iii. page 155, fig. 19), but the shell is much larger. The parietal armature further connects it with the species just named, but the palatal armature is more like that of *P. leiophis.* The two specimens of the new species are stated by Miss Linter to be from Thayet-Mayo, Pegu, Burma; a third specimen, which is in Miss Linter's collection, is accompanied by a label bearing the locality, Niningo (Burma?), but I have failed to trace this name in any of the maps and gazetteers to which I have access.

The specimen figured, and the one in Miss Linter's collection, have the measurements given in the diagnosis, but my second specimen measures only 12·5 millimetres in diameter. Figs. 67*a-c* show the shell in three different aspects, natural size; figs. 67*d-f*, are enlarged; *d*, shows the

and round the umbilicus, and descending shortly and abruptly in front. Aperture heart-shaped; peristome white, scarcely thickened, a little reflected; the margins united by an elevated sinuous ridge on the parietal callus, notched at the lower junction. Umbilicus wide and deep. Parietal wall with a thin vertical plate, strongly deflected posteriorly below, and giving off a short horizontal ridge at the upper extremity on each side; a long horizontal flexuous fold rises close to the upper extremity of this plate on the anterior side, descending suddenly at first, then ascending gradually, and afterwards gradually descending, following the deflection of the last whorl, becoming united to the ridge at the aperture; a second, shorter, horizontal fold occurs below this one, rising close to the lower extremity of the vertical plate, proceeding horizontally at first, and then ascending a little; another very thin fold rises below the vertical plate, running parallel to the lower suture as far as the aperture, where it unites with the ridge. Palatal folds, five: the first, rather long and thin, near to and parallel with the suture, with a deep indentation near the posterior extremity, dividing it into two unequal parts; the second, horizontal, a little deflected posteriorly, with an elongated denticle posteriorly, and a second, smaller, one above the first; the third fold much shorter, strongly curved downwards posteriorly, with a minute denticle posteriorly; the fourth fold vertical with an obliquely descending ridge posteriorly at the upper extremity, and bifurcated at the lower extremity, the anterior arm of the bifurcation the shorter; a minute denticle occurs near the ridge at the upper extremity and a second one near the middle, both on the posterior side; the fifth fold is thin, horizontal, and strongly deflected on both sides.—Major diameter, 15 millimetres; minor diameter, 12 millimetres; altitude, 5 millimetres.—Habitat, Thayet-Mayo, Pegu, Burma.—Type in my collection.

ARMATURE OF HELICOID LANDSHELLS,

WITH A NEW SPECIES OF PLECTOPYLIS.

BY G. K. GUDE, F.Z.S.

(*Continued from page 232.*)

PLECTOPYLIS OGLEI (figs. 68a-h), from Sadiya, Assam, was described and figured by Lieut.-Colonel Godwin-Austen in the "Journal of the Asiatic Society of Bengal," xlviii. (1879), p. 3, t. 1, f. 2. The shell is dextral, disk-shaped, widely umbilicated, corneous, marked transversely

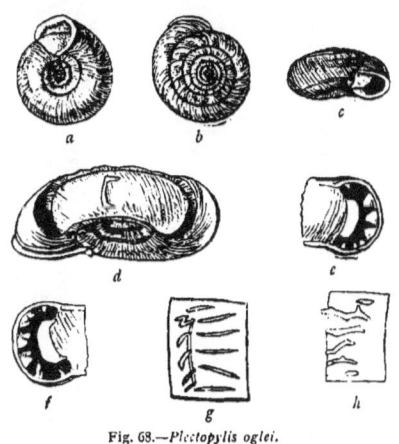

Fig. 68.—*Plectopylis oglei.*

with dark brown, finely and closely striated, the upper side coarsely decussated with raised spiral lines. The spire is scarcely raised, the apex a little elevated, and the suture impressed. There are eight rounded whorls, which increase slowly and regularly, the last being angular above and below, and obsoletely keeled at the periphery, descending slowly in front. The aperture is oblique, roundly ovate, slightly depressed above; the peristome is white, thickened and reflexed, its margins are connected by a scarcely raised curved ridge on the parietal callus, a slight notch being observable above and below at the junctions. The parietal armature consists of a single strong vertical plate, which gives off posteriorly two short ridges, one at the upper and one at the lower extremity (see fig. 68d, which gives an enlarged view of a specimen with the outer wall removed). The palatal armature consists of six horizontal folds: the first, near the suture, very short and thin; the second, third, fourth, fifth, and sixth, bilobed or bisected about the middle, where a slight vertical ridge connects their posterior portions; the posterior portion of the second fold is sinuous,

somewhat S-shaped; the third, fourth, and fifth are slightly deflected posteriorly; the sixth is very unequally bisected, the posterior portion being less than a third the length of the anterior portion, which is raised at first and then suddenly deflected (see fig. 68g, which shows the inside of the outer wall of the shell enlarged). The illustrations have been made from the type specimens in the collection of Lieut.-Colonel Godwin-Austen, to whom I am under obligation for the loan of them. The specimen shown in figs. 68a-c (natural size) measures: major diameter, 27 millimetres; minor diameter, 25 millimetres; altitude, 8 millimetres; figs. 68e-g (enlarged), are taken from a specimen not quite full-grown; e shows the parietal and palatal armatures from the anterior side; f, their posterior aspect; and g, as just mentioned, the inside of the outer wall with its folds. This specimen exhibits the remains of a previous parietal plate, one quarter of a whorl behind the permanent one. Fig. 68h, shows the inside of a portion of the outer shell-wall of the specimen shown in fig. 68d, the armature of which is incomplete, a portion having been broken away. Two immature specimens in different stages of growth exhibit armatures identical in all respects with those illustrated, except that the palatal folds are less bilobed. The species under consideration is allied to *Plectopylis serica*, but it is larger, and presents considerable differences in the palatal armature.

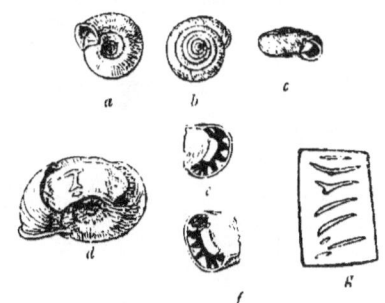

Fig. 69.—*Plectopylis munipurensis.*

Plectopylis munipurensis (figs. 69a-g), from the Ihang Valley, Munipur, was described and figured by Lieut.-Col. Godwin-Austen in the "Proceedings of the Zoological Society," 1874, p. 610, t. 73, f. 6.

The shell is dextral, disk-shaped, deeply and rather widely umbilicated, pale ochreous brown, irregularly marked with a darker shade, regularly and finely striated, with many raised spiral ridges. The spire is depressed-conical, the apex prominent, and the suture slightly impressed. There are seven whorls, flattened above and tumid below, the last scarcely descending in front. The aperture is oblique, a little depressed above, somewhat ear-shaped; the peristome is white, a little thickened and reflexed, its margins being united by a strong, raised, curved ridge on the parietal callus, and notched above and below at the junctions. The parietal armature consists of a single, strong, vertical plate, which is obliquely deflected towards the aperture; it has two slight supports posteriorly —the lower a little deflected, the upper obliquely raised—and gives off anteriorly, at the upper extremity, a long, slightly raised ridge; a minute denticle occurs just below the vertical plate (see fig. 69*d*, which gives an enlarged view of the shell with a portion of the outer wall removed). The palatal armature consists of six more or less horizontal folds: the first very minute near the suture; the second long and descending a little obliquely towards the middle, with the posterior end suddenly raised; the third and fourth also descending a little obliquely, their posterior extremities dilated, almost bifurcated; the fifth also descending a little, its posterior termination suddenly deflected; the sixth, horizontal, with a minute denticle above, and an elongated one a little further back, below the posterior termination of the fold (see fig. 69*g*, which shows the inside of the outer wall of the shell). The figures are taken from the type specimens in the collection of Lieut.-Colonel Godwin-Austen, who has obligingly lent them to me for this purpose. The shell measures: major diameter, 10·5-11 millimetres; minor diameter, 9-9·5 millimetres; altitude, 5 millimetres. Figs. 69*a-c* are of natural size, while figs. 69*d-g* are enlarged; *e* shows the armatures from the anterior and *f* from the posterior side.

Plectopylis blanda ([1]) (figs. 70*a-f*). A single speci-

men received by the writer under the name of *Plectopylis minor*, from the Naga Hills, was sent to Lieut.-Colonel Godwin-Austen for examination, and was found by him to be a new species. It differs from *Plectopylis minor* in being larger and more elevated, and having a wider and deeper umbilicus. The parietal armature differs in having an additional fold above the vertical plate, and the anterior denticles are almost united to this fold. The palatal armature differs in the posterior folds being very short and almost reduced to denticles. Figs. 70*a-c* show the shell in three

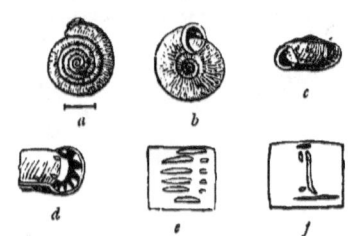

Fig. 70.—*Plectopylis blanda.*

different aspects. Fig. 70*d* gives the posterior view of the two armatures; *e*, the inside of the outer wall; and *f*, a portion of the parietal wall, with its plate and folds. All the figures are enlarged.

Erratum. -- A typographical error occurs *ante* p. 231—the name *Plectopylis leucochilus* should read *Plectopylis leucochila.*

(*To be continued.*)

([1]) *Plectopylis blanda,* n. sp. (figs. 70*a-f*).—Shell sinistral, depressed conical, widely and deeply umbilicated, whitish-corneous, finely and regularly ribbed. Spire conical, apex prominent, suture distinctly impressed. Whorls six, tumid above, rounded below, increasing very slowly and regularly, the last not descending in front, angulated above the periphery and round the wide perspective umbilicus. The cuticle is produced into deciduous hairs on the ribs, forming spiral rows. Aperture oblique, lunate, a little flattened on the upper, outer margin. Peristome white, a little thickened and reflexed, the margins united by a slight, flexuous ridge on the parietal callus. Parietal wall with a strong, vertical plate, slightly deflected anteriorly and having two minute denticles posteriorly, the upper vertically the lower horizontally elongated. A very thin horizontal fold occurs below the vertical plate and a very short fold above it. Palatal folds in two series; the anterior consisting of six thin horizontal folds, the first and sixth a little shorter and placed a little further back than the other four; the posterior series consists of four very short folds or denticles.—Major diameter, 6 millimetres; minor diameter, 5 millimetres; altitude, 3 millimetres. Habitat—Naga Hills, Assam.—Type in my collection.

ARMATURE OF HELICOID LANDSHELLS,

WITH A NEW FORM OF PLECTOPYLIS.

BY G. K. GUDE, F.Z.S.

(Continued from page 264.)

PLECTOPYLIS DIPTYCHIA (figs. 71*a-f*), from the province of Konei-Tchou, China, was described by Dr. von Möllendorff in the "Jahrbuch der Deutschen Malakozoologischen Gesellschaft," xii (1885), p. 390, and the shell was figured in the same work, t. 10, f. 17. No figure of the armature, as far as I have been able to ascertain, has hitherto been published; my readers will, therefore, be glad to be able to form an idea of these structures from the accompanying figures. The shell is dextral, discoid, light corneous, thin, sub-pellucid, finely striated, decussated with microscopic spiral lines above, shining below, widely and deeply umbilicated. The cuticle is produced into distant plaits, which are very prominent at the periphery. The spire is a little raised, and the suture is impressed. There are six narrow whorls, which increase slowly and regularly, the last is angulated above the periphery, rounded below, not deflected in front. The aperture is roundly lunate, oblique; the peristome white, a little thickened and reflexed, the margins scarcely united by the parietal callus, which is devoid of any ridge at the aperture. The parietal armature consists of two strong vertical plates, slightly converging above; the anterior one curved, with the convex side towards the aperture, giving off anteriorly at the upper extremity a short horizontal ridge, and being a little deflected

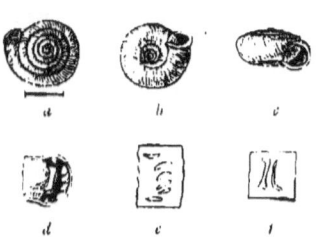

Fig. 71.—*Plectopylis diptychia.*

posteriorly below. The posterior one is crescent-shaped, strongly deflected posteriorly below (see fig. 71*f*, which shows the parietal wall of the shell with its two plates). The palatal armature is composed of six short, more or less horizontal folds; the first very minute, near the suture; the second, third, fourth and fifth obliquely deflected posteriorly; the sixth horizontal (see fig. 71*e*, which shows the inside of the outer shell-wall with its folds). The specimen figured measures: major

diameter, 6 millimetres; minor diameter, 5 millimetres; altitude, 3 millimetres. It was sent to me by Dr. von Möllendorff, and is now in my collection. All the figures are enlarged.

Plectopylis murata (figs. 72*a* and *b*), from Tchen-K'eou, China, was described and figured by Mr. Heude, in Part 2 of his "Notes sur les Mollusques terrestres de la Vallée du Fleuve Bleu" (1885), p. 112, t. 30, f. 1. The shell is dextral, discoid,

Fig. 72.—*Plectopylis murata.*

light corneous, finely striated and decussated with microscopic spiral lines above, smooth and shining below. On the upper side, the cuticle is produced into distant persisting plaits, which form a coarse fringe around the periphery. The spire is a little elevated, and the suture linear. There are five and a-half to six whorls, which increase regularly, and are flattened above and rounded below; the last does not descend in front, and is keeled at the periphery. The aperture is rounded, oblique; the peristome white, a little thickened and reflexed, its margins being united by a slight ridge on the parietal callus; the umbilicus is wide and deep. The parietal armature is similar to that of *Plectopylis stenochila* (see my note in this series of papers, SCIENCE-GOSSIP, N.S., Vol. iii. p. 204, figs. 29*b* and *d*), and is as variable as in that species. The number of denticles in front of the vertical plate in *Plectopylis murata* varies from one to three, or such denticles may be absent altogether, while the upper and lower short horizontal folds in front of the vertical plate, may be reduced to denticles. The palatal armature is also similar to that of *Plectopylis stenochila* (loc. cit. figs. 29*c* and *d*), to which species the present one is closely allied, but the shell is more depressed, and the whorls are flattened above with the base shining and translucent, while in *Plectopylis stenochila* the whorls are rounded above with the base striated and opaque. In the species under consideration there are only five and a-half to six whorls, and the umbilicus is more widened at the last whorl, which is keeled at the periphery, and the fimbriae are coarser, longer and more persistent. The specimen shown in figs. 72 *a* and *b*, from Sse-Tchuan, China, is one of two sent to me by Dr. von Möllendorff; it measures: major diameter, 7·5 millimetres; minor diameter 6·5 millimetres; altitude, 3·75 millimetres.

Plectopylis trochospira (figs. 73*a-c*), from Mount Licos, Cebu, Philippine Islands, was described by Dr. von Möllendorff in the "Jahrbuch der Deutschen Malakazoologischen Gesellschaft," xiv. (1887), p. 273, and the shell was figured in the same work, t. 8, f. 9. The armature, however, was not illustrated, and I believe the figures now given are the first which have appeared. The shell is dextral, widely and deeply umbilicated, depressed-conical, light corneous, finely ribbed above and striated below. The spire is conical and the suture impressed. There are six narrow rounded whorls, which increase slowly and regularly; the last, considerably wider than the penultimate, has a thread-like keel at the periphery, is angulated round the umbilicus and does not descend in front. The aperture is diagonal, lunate; the peristome white, a little thickened and reflexed, the margins being slightly convergent and united by a scarcely raised sinuous ridge at the parietal callus. The parietal armature consists of two long, parallel, horizontal folds, which revolve over nearly half a whorl, the upper one being the stronger and united to the ridge at the aperture, while the lower one is thinner

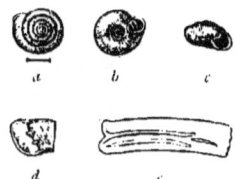

Fig. 73.—*Plectopylis trochospira.*

and terminates at a short distance from the ridge; a very thin, short horizontal fold occurs posteriorly a little below the upper fold (see fig. 73*c*, which shows the parietal wall of the shell with its folds). The palatal armature is composed of five short, thin, horizontal folds, which descend a little anteriorly (see fig. 73*d*, which shows both the parietal and the palatal armatures from the posterior side). The specimen figured is in the collection of Professor Oscar Boettger, of Frankfort, by whom this shell—which measures: major diameter, 4 millimetres; minor diameter, 3·5 millimetres; altitude, 2 millimetres—was obligingly lent to me.

Plectopylis trochospira is allied to *P. quadrasi* (*ante* p. 71, f. 54), but it is larger and much lighter in colour; there are also certain differences in the armature.

Plectopylis trochospira, var. *boholensis*([1]). Two specimens kindly lent to me by Mr. Ponsonby, labelled with the manuscript name, "*Plectopylis trochospira*

Fig. 74.—*Plectopylis trochospira* var. *boholensis.*

var. *boholensis* (Möllendorff)," certainly represent a distinct variety. They are smaller than the type, and the umbilicus is narrower. The armature is nearly identical, but the palatal folds are connected at their posterior terminations by a very slight transverse sinuous ridge, plainly discernible externally through the shell-wall.

(*To be continued.*)

(1) *Plectopylis trochospira* var. *boholensis*, n. var. (fig. 74). differs from the type in being smaller and having a narrower umbilicus. Major diameter, 3·25 millimetres; minor diameter, 3 millimetres; altitude, 1·75 millimetres. Habitat, Bohol Island, Philippine Islands. Type in Mr. Ponsonby's collection.

ARMATURE OF HELICOID LANDSHELLS.

By G. K. Gude, F.Z.S.

(Continued from Vol. iv. p. 285).

A FEW more species of *Plectopylis* remain to be described and figured. Their consideration has been delayed on account of authentic specimens being inaccessible to me; in one case no figures have yet been published, while in another case, where the species is supposed to have been illustrated, the figures represent another form. These are *Plectopylis repercussa*, *P. anguina*, and *P. refuga*, all described by Dr. A. A. Gould. In the present instalment I will discuss *P. refuga* together with *P. leiophis*, which has been confused with it in some quarters, leaving *P. repercussa* and *P. anguina*, and sundry other allied species for consideration in future instalments of these papers. *Plectopylis repercussa* has recently been regarded as synonymous with *P. achatina*, but whether justly so or not, it was

p. 99. This species has not hitherto been illustrated, as the figures given by Philippi, by Reeve, and by Küster were taken from the specimens in Cuming's collection, now in the British Museum, and these specimens, although labelled *P. refuga*, are not that species, but *P. leiophis*, as careful comparison with Mr. Benson's type specimens has convinced me. I have been unable to obtain any specimens of *P. refuga*, and I am therefore compelled to rely upon Dr. Gould's description, supplemented by the notes and sketches by Dr. Bagg, and by the photographs now reproduced. Dr. Gould described the shell as "sinistrorse, discoid, flat above, concave below, greenish-corneous; whorls, six, closely coiled, thickly striated, the last deflexed near the aperture;

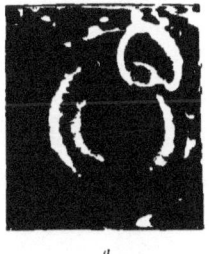 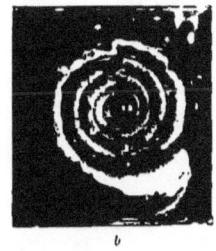 

a   b

 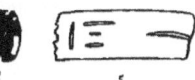

d   e

Fig. 75.—*Plectopylis refuga.*

impossible for me to decide, as the type specimens of the former, as well as of the other two species, are in the possession of the New York State Museum, Albany, N.Y., and my request for the loan of them was referred to the Trustees, who decided not to let the specimens go out of the country. The Director, Dr. Merrill, however, very obligingly had the shells photographed and their armatures sketched for me. I have thus the pleasure of being able to lay authentic figures before my readers. I am much indebted to Dr. Merrill, as well as to Dr. Bagg, his assistant, who made the sketches and furnished valuable notes, which, together with the photographs, enabled me to clear up the doubtful points in connection with the three species in question.

Plectopylis refuga (figs. 75a-e), from Tavoy, Burma, was described by Dr. Gould in the "Proceedings of the Boston Natural History Society," ii. (1846),

suture impressed; aperture very oblique, heart-shaped; peristome white, reflexed, connected by a sinuous callus; a white flexuous plate revolving in the penultimate whorl." He further remarks that "this remarkable shell is almost exactly like *Helix carabinata*, Fer. [*Corilla rivolii*, Desh.], except that it is reversed, and has no lamellae revolving within the outer lip." From the above description it is impossible to know which form Dr. Gould had before him, as it applies equally to several distinct shells.

The following notes have been communicated by Dr. Bagg: "*Helix refuga*, Gould, catalogue number, 271; original number, A 562. Two earliest volutions smooth, remainder of shell very finely striate and hairy. Outer volution on lower side angular. Greater diameter nearly ¾ inch = 19 millimetres; smaller diameter, ⁹⁄₁₆ inch = 14 millimetres; altitude, $\frac{3}{32}$ inch [= 4 millimetres]; length of horizontal fold at aperture, $\frac{3}{16}$ inch [= 5 millimetres]. Basal denticle [*i.e.* vertical parietal plate] cup-shaped."

From figs. 75*d* and *e*, which have been copied from Dr. Bagg's sketches, it appears that the parietal armature consists of a strong vertical plate which is concave posteriorly; on the posterior side there are three short horizontal folds, the upper longest, the median shortest; a short horizontal fold at the aperture is united to the flexuous ridge (see fig. 75*e*, which shows the parietal wall); while the palatal armature appears to consist of six folds: the first three short and horizontal; the fourth strong, vertical, slightly indented about the middle; the fifth and sixth horizontal and thin (see fig. 75*d*, which gives the posterior aspect of both armatures). Figs. 75*a-c* are reproduced from the photographs of the type specimens, enlarged two diameters. Mr. W. T. Blanford has recorded the following additional habitats for this species: Pegu and Tenasserim (in "British Burma Gazetteer" (1879), i. p. 709).

Plectopylis leiophis (figs. 76*a-c*) from Thayet Myo, Pegu, was described by Mr. Benson in the

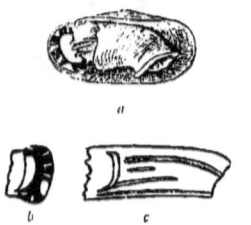

a

b   *c*

Fig. 76. *Plectopylis leiophis.*

"Annals and Magazine of Natural History" (3), v. (1860), p. 246, and illustrated by Lieut.-Colonel Godwin-Austen in the "Proceedings of the Zoological Society," 1874, t. 74, fig. 2, who subsequently (*ibid.* 1875, p. 44) stated that this shell was identical with Dr. Gould's *P. refuga*, basing this identification on the specimens in the British Museum, so labelled by Mr. Cuming. Upon comparing these latter with Mr. Benson's type specimens, obligingly lent to me by Mr. Harmer, of the University Museum of Zoology, Cambridge, I found they were certainly identical, but as already stated, the specimens in the British Museum were wrongly identified. They formed the subject of the illustrations purporting to represent *P. refuga* in Dr. R. A. Philippi's "Beschreibungen und Abbildungen neuer oder wenig gekannter Conchylien," iii. Helix, t. 10, f. 4; in Reeve's "Conchologia Iconica," t. 82, f. 436, and in "Martini und Chemnitz, Conchylien Cabinet" (2), i. t. 66, ff. 21-23. All these figures,

therefore, must be referred to *P. leiophis*. This species was also figured in Hanley and Theobald's "Conchologia Indica," t. 13, f. 8. In addition to the original habitat, the species has been found at Kivadouk, and Akoutoung on the Irawady, below Prome (W. T. Blanford, Journ. As. Soc., Bengal, xxxiv. (1865), p. 75). I very much doubt that Mr. Benson was acquainted with *Plectopylis refuga*, although Mr. Blanford believes he knew the species. Mr. Benson, in discussing *P. leiophis* (Ann. Mag. Nat. Hist. (3), v. (1860), p. 246), mentions, it is true, *P. refuga* var *dextrorsa*, but this form, as has already been shown, is allied to *P. brachydiscus* (*c.f.* SCIENCE-GOSSIP, iii. p. 154) and is quite distinct from *P. refuga* and *P. leiophis*. A specimen in the McAndrew Collection, in the University Museum of Zoology at Cambridge, which contains Mr. Benson's types, is labelled *P. refuga*, but I refer this without hesitation to a form of *P. achatina*. *P. leiophis* is sinistral, discoid, pale rufous-corneous, finely and regularly striated, decussated by microscopic spiral lines on the upper surface, spirally wrinkled at the side and below. The spire is depressed, the apex raised a little above the plane of the other whorls, and the suture impressed. There are six and a-half narrow rounded whorls, which increase very slowly and regularly; the last being angulated above the periphery, shortly and abruptly descending in front, widening a little towards the aperture, and slightly constricted behind the peristome. The aperture is roundly cordate, oblique; the peristome white, thickened and reflected; the margins converging and united by a raised curved ridge on the parietal callus, slightly notched at the lower junction. The umbilicus is wide and moderately deep. The parietal armature consists of a strong vertical plate, angular above, where it gives off posteriorly an abruptly descending short ridge, while below it deflects obliquely, and on the anterior side it gives off a short horizontal fold; a long free horizontal fold rises close to the vertical plate a little below its upper extremity, revolving parallel with the whorl as far as the aperture, where it unites with the ridge on the parietal callus; between this fold and the lower one just referred to, occurs a very short, free, horizontal fold, but this does not appear to be constant, as it is absent in a specimen in Mr. Blanford's collection, while in an immature specimen in my collection, it appears as two small coalesced folds, and in this instance an additional elongated denticle occurs between it and the upper long fold; in all the other specimens examined, however, the parietal armature is identical with that of the type specimen. A very thin, free horizontal fold rises below the vertical plate, running close to the lower suture, and terminating close to the ridge at the aperture. The palatal armature is composed of six folds, five horizontal and one sub-vertical ; the first is thin, horizontal, parallel with and near to the suture, slightly indented about a third of its length from the posterior termination ; the second stouter and longer, also horizontal, slightly depressed, and indented near its posterior termination ; the third stout, horizontal, but shorter than the first, also indented near the posterior extremity ; the fourth, stout, horizontal, shorter than the third, bluntly triangular, the apex reflexed, and having a slightly elongated thin denticle posteriorly in a line with it ; the fifth, stout and very short, sub-vertical, obliquely crescent-shaped, the concave side towards the aperture and lower suture ; on the posterior side, near the lower extremity, occurs a small denticle ; the sixth is short, but broad, horizontal, and it has an elongated dentical posteriorly. The specimen figured is in Mr. Ponsonby's collection, and is from Pegu. It measures : major diameter, 13·5 millimetres ; minor diameter, 11·5 millimetres ; altitude, 5 millimetres. Two specimens in my collection, from Akoutoung, are a little more raised in the spire and less angular above the periphery ; they measure 14 millimetres in diameter ; altitude, 6 millimetres.

An immature specimen in my collection, having five and a-half whorls completed, is interesting from the fact that it possesses the set of barriers nearly identical with that of mature specimens ; but the upper horizontal parietal fold is very short, only about one quarter of the length of that in old specimens, the anterior portion being absent ; the thin lowest fold runs as far as the aperture. As already mentioned, the second fold appears as two coalesced folds, and an additional denticle occurs between it and the upper fold.

ADDENDUM. — *Plectopylis pseudophis* (figs. 77*a* and *b*).—Since writing my remarks upon this species (vol. iv., p. 170, f. 62), I have been fortunate in obtaining a specimen through the kindness of the Rev. R. Ashington Bullen. I am thus able to supplement my former notes and figures, which were copied from other sources, as at that time I had not examined the armature. · The specimen in question differs from the type of *P. pseudophis*, as described by Lieut.-Colonel Godwin Austen, in having an additional short fold between the long upper and the short lower parietal fold, resembling in this respect *P. leiophis*; but as already stated, when discussing that species, this character appears to be an inconstant one. The palatal armature consists of : first, a short thin horizontal fold near the suture ; secondly, a longer horizontal fold, somewhat deflected posteriorly, with an additional short wedge-like fold attached to it, which has posteriorly, a little above it, a small denticle ; thirdly, a shorter horizontal fold widened towards the posterior extremity, then suddenly attenuated and indented, and finally

again widened a little ; fourthly. a short, slightly curved horizontal fold, descending a little posteriorly, also slightly attenuated and indented near the posterior extremity ; fifthly, a crescent-shaped, sub-vertical fold (the concave side being towards the aperture and the lower suture), with a small denticle near its posterior extremity ; and sixthly,

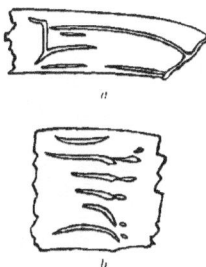

Fig. 77.—*Plectopylis pseudophis*.

a longer curved horizontal fold, having its upper edge reflected towards the fifth fold, and possessing a small denticle near its posterior extremity.

(*To be continued.*)

ARMATURE OF HELICOID LANDSHELLS.

By G. K. Gude, F.Z.S.

(Continued from p. 17.)

PLECTOPYLIS repercussa (figs. 78*a–i*), from Tavoy, Burma, was described by Dr. Gould in the "Proceedings of the Boston Society of Natural History," vi. (1856), p. 11 ; but as the diagnosis is somewhat vague and as the species was not illustrated, subsequent authors have considered it to be synonymous with *P. achatina*, from which species, however, it differs in outward appearance as well as in its armature. The shell is sinistrorse, disk-shaped, pale corneous, finely striated, the upper raised flexuous ridge, slightly notched above and below at the junctions. The parietal armature is very complicated, being of the same type as in *Plectopylis karenorum*, described and illustrated in this series of papers (SCIENCE-GOSSIP, N.S. iii. Feb. 1897, p. 245, f. 35). These two species, together with *Plectopylis achatina, P. anguina* and *P. linterae*, to be considered afterwards, form a distinct group, connected with the group of *P. ponsonbyi* by a transition form, represented by a single

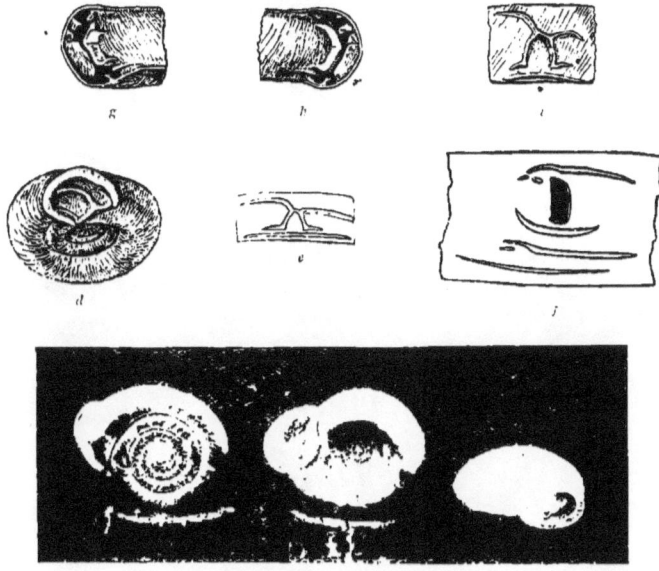

Fig. 78.—*Plectopylis repercussa.*

side being strongly decussated by spiral lines, almost obsolete at the side, but reappearing in the umbilical region. The spire is a little raised, the suture linear. There are seven regularly coiled whorls, which increase slowly and gradually, and are flattened above and tumid below. The last whorl is tricarinated, one keel being at the periphery, one above, and another below (in young shells these keels are provided with a fringe of coarse hairs); this whorl widens suddenly at the aperture, where it is deeply deflected. The aperture is almost horizontal, elliptic cordate; the peristome white, thickened, and strongly reflected; the margins united by a

specimen as yet undescribed, received by me from Mr. Robert Cairns, of Hurst, Ashton-under-Lyne. A long, stout, horizontal median fold, given off at the apertural ridge, proceeds parallel with the last whorl for a quarter of the length of that whorl, when it gives off a shortly descending, slightly reflected arm, provided anteriorly at the lower extremity with a short, abruptly descending horizontal ridge; the fold then rises obliquely for a short distance, and finally bifurcates ; *the lower arm of the bifurcation the shorter*, and descending almost vertically; it is provided posteriorly with a short horizontal ridge at its

lower extremity; the upper arm at first ascends obliquely, then proceeds horizontally close to the suture, and gradually attenuates. Below these complicated structures, there is a free, thin, horizontal fold close to and parallel with the lower suture, and extending from the aperture to a little beyond the lower arm of the bifurcation and its posterior support (see fig. 78e, which shows part of the parietal wall). At the aperture this fold is *distinctly united to the transverse sinuous ridge* (see fig. 78d). The palatal armature consists of: first, a strong long horizontal fold near the suture and parallel with it, as well as with the posterior portion of the upper arm of the parietal bifurcation, with which it terminates at the same point posteriorly; secondly, a shorter, but much stronger and broader horizontal fold, which deflects with a

terior half, with the concave side facing the vertical plate (see fig. 78f, enlarged, which shows the inner side of the palatal wall with its folds and denticles). Figs. 78g–i (also enlarged) show an immature specimen of five and a-half whorls, in Mr. Ponsonby's collection; the armature is almost identical with that of the mature specimens, but the main median parietal fold is very short and does not rise from the aperture, while the denticle in front of the lower part of the palatal vertical plate is very strongly developed, and it is united to the plate, so as to form a steep ridge. A second set of barriers, identical in every respect except in being a little smaller, occurs in this specimen one-quarter of a whorl further back. The mature specimen shown in fig. 78d is also in the collection of Mr. Ponsonby, and measures: major diameter, 31 milli-

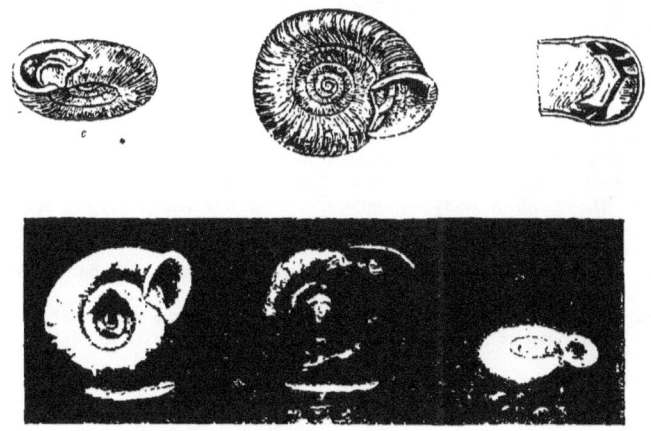

Fig. 79.— *Plectopylis anguina.*

sharp curve posteriorly, having a little above its posterior termination, and almost in a line with its anterior portion, a slight elongated horizontal denticle; thirdly, a very short, but strong and broad crescent-shaped fold, deflected at both extremities; fourthly, facing the concave side of the last-mentioned fold, is a very strong and broad vertical plate, strongly inclined towards the aperture, with a much reflexed and thickened edge; this plate intercalates between the two lower arms of the parietal armature; on the posterior side of the plate and near its lower extremity occurs a stout little denticle, and a little lower and still farther back is found a slight elongated swelling, not amounting to a fold or denticle (yet present in all four mature specimens, as well as in an immature one, examined by me); fifthly, a thin horizontal fold, the anterior part straight, but curved in the pos-

metres; minor diameter, 24 millimetres; altitude, 9 millimetres; while the immature specimen measures 17 millimetres in diameter. Three specimens in my collection measure respectively 29 : 23 : 9 millimetres, 25 : 20 : 8·5 millimetres, 23 : 18 : 7·5 millimetres. The types of the species are in the New York State Museum, at Albany, N.Y., and are shown in figs. 78a–c, which are reproduced from the photograph kindly supplied by Dr. Merrill. The following particulars are taken from Dr. Bagg's notes which accompanied the photographs: "*Helix repercussa*, Gould. Burmah. Catalogue No., 236; original No., A 564. Major diameter, 1⅛ inch [= 28·5 millimetres]; minor diameter, ⅞ inch [= 22 millimetres]; altitude, 5/16 inch [= 8 millimetres]; greatest diameter of aperture, 7/16 inch [= 11 millimetres]." Dr. Gould states that the species was taken in the

Mergui Archipelago, but as this has never been confirmed it may be assumed that the collector, the Rev. J. Benjamin, made a mistake as to the locality. Mr. W. T. Blanford gives also the following localities : Moulmain and Tenasserim (in " British Burma Gazetteer," 1879, i. p. 709).

Plectopylis anguina (figs. 79*a-f*), from Tavoy, Burma, was described by Dr. Gould in the " Proceedings of the Boston Natural History Society," ii. (1847), p. 218 ; and it was figured in Hanley and Theobald's " Conchologia Indica," t. 13, f. 7. By some authorities this species has been considered identical with *P. achatina.* It appears, however, to be perfectly distinct. The shell is sinistral, much flattened, discoid, varying in colour from corneous to dark chestnut ; below it is usually paler and flammulated with dark chestnut ; it is finely striated and decussated by microscopic spiral lines. The spire is depressed, the suture linear. There are five and a-half regularly coiled whorls, which increase slowly and gradually ; they are a little flattened above and a little rounded below. The last whorl is slightly angulated at the periphery ; it widens rather suddenly at the aperture, and is deeply deflected in front, and somewhat constricted behind the peristome. The umbilicus is extremely shallow; in a specimen in my collection it is only 1·5 milli-metre in depth. The aperture is nearly horizontal, cordate ; the peristome is livid or pale brown, a little thickened and much reflexed. A sinuous raised ridge on the parietal wall at the aperture connects the margins of the peristome; at the junctions above and below, however, there are slight notches. The armature is similar in most respects to that of *P. repercussa*, but it is less solid and heavy, the *lower* arm of the bifurcation on the parietal wall is *longer* than the upper, and the thin free horizontal fold near the lower suture is not united to the ridge at the aperture and *does not proceed beyond the lower arm of the bifurcation,* as it does in *P. repercussa.* The upper fold of the palatal armature is much shorter than in *P. repercussa*, terminating posteriorly at the same point as the shorter upper arm of the parietal bifurcation ; the second and fifth horizontal palatal folds are much shorter anteriorly than in *P. repercussa* ; while the vertical palatal plate (the fourth) is broader, but less stout and less inclined towards the aperture than is the case in that species. The specimen shown in figs. 79*d* and *e* is from Moulmain, and is in my collection. It measures : major diameter, 28 millimetres ; minor diameter, 22 millimetres ; altitude, 7·5 millimetres. Mr. Blanford has also recorded the species from Tenasserim (" British Burma Gazetteer " (1879), i. p. 709), while Mr. Nevill mentions Kuengan ("Hand-list," p. 72). Mr. Ponsonby possesses two specimens from Sgwagakin, Salween Valley, measuring 25 milli-metres in diameter. Figs. 79*a-c* are reproduced from photographs of Dr. Gould's type specimens in the New York State Museum. Dr. Bagg has supplied the following notes respecting them : " *Helix anguina,* Gould. Catalogue No., 251 ; original No., A 558. The shell is somewhat banded by brownish and white alternating, but not in all specimens." Fig. 79*f* shows the posterior aspect of the parietal and palatal armatures.

(*To be continued.*)

ARMATURE OF HELICOID LANDSHELLS
AND NEW FORMS OF PLECTOPYLIS.

BY G. K. GUDE, F.Z.S.

(*Continued from page 76.*)

PLECTOPYLIS *achatina* (figs. 80*a–f*, 81*a–d* and 82*a–c*), from Moulmain, Burma, was described by. Dr. Pfeiffer, in the " Zeitschrift für Malakozoologie," 1845, p. 86, and Mr. Benson gave notes on the animal, in the " Annals and Magazine

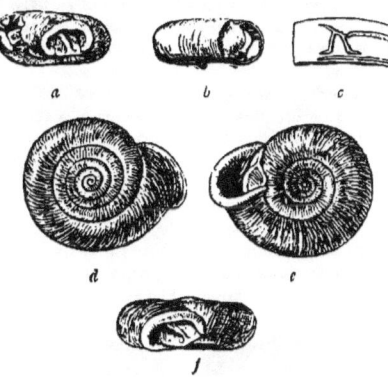

a   *b*   *c*

d   *e*

f

Fig. 80.—*Plectopylis achatina.*

of Natural History" (3), iv. (1859), p. 95. The shell was figured in Hanley and Theobald's " Conchologia Indica," t. 13, f. 1 and 4 (the latter figure purporting to represent *P. repercussa.*) Mr. Stoliczka described and figured the anatomy of the animal in the " Journal of the Asiatic Society of Bengal," xl. (1871), p. 221, t. 15, f. 1–3, and Lieut.-Colonel Godwin-Austen, the parietal armature of the shell in the "Proceedings of the Zoological Society," 1874, t. 74, f. 6. The shell is sinistrorse, disk-shaped, very widely umbilicated, of various shades of chestnut, usually paler and sometimes flammulated below, irregularly and finely striated. The apex is usually, but not invariably, raised slightly above the plane of the whorls. There are six or six and a-half whorls, which increase gradually, and are more or less flattened above and tumid below ; the first three and a-half are smooth or nearly so, while the next two are somewhat coarsely striated and strongly decussated by spiral lines, less distinct on the upper side of the last whorl, obsolete at its side, but reappearing in the umbilical region. The last whorl is bluntly keeled above and sub-angulated at the periphery ; this whorl suddenly widens at the aperture where it is deeply deflected. The aperture is almost horizontal,

elliptic cordate, while the peristome is thickened and strongly reflected, livid or purplish-brown in colour, *never white ;* the margins are united by a raised sinuous ridge, slightly notched at the junctions above and below. The parietal armature is of the same type as that of *P. repercussa (ante* p. 74, f. 78*c*), but *the lower arm of the bifurcation is the longer of the two* (see fig. 80*c*, which shows part of the parietal wall with the posterior portion of its armature), and the lower free horizontal fold close to the lower suture *does not reach as far as the apertural ridge, and does not extend beyond the lower arm of the bifurcation and its posterior support.* Fig. 80*a* gives the anterior and fig. 80*b* the posterior aspect of both armatures. The palatal armature is also similar to that of *P. repercussa,* but the first horizontal fold is shorter in the present species correspondingly with the reduction in the upper arm of the bifurcation of the parietal armature, while the vertical plate is less strong and its edge less thickened. *Plectopylis repercussa* is, generally speaking, a more solid and larger shell, always lighter in colour than *P. achatina,* while its white peristome will at once distinguish it from the latter species. The lower horizontal parietal fold in *P. repercussa* is always distinctly united to the apertural ridge, whereas in *P. achatina* this fold is not visible from the aperture. That these characters are constant, I have reason to believe from having opened sixteen or eighteen specimens without finding any variation in these respects. The specimen shown in figs. 80*a* and *b* measures : major diameter, 22 millimetres ; minor

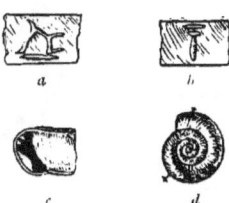

a   *b*

c   *d*

Fig. 81.—*Plectopylis achatina juv.*

diameter, 17 millimetres ; altitude, 7 millimetres ; while the one shown in figs. 80*d–f* measures 27 : 21 : 8 millimetres ; both are from Moulmain, and are in my collection. Another specimen in my collection shows no trace of the ridge at the aperture, but is in all other respects like the mature shells. In figs. 81a-d I have shown an immature shell, received from Mr. J. E. Cooper, of Highgate; it has only four whorls completed, and is only furnished with the posterior portion of the parietal armature (see fig. 81a), but the palatal armature is quite complete, though correspondingly reduced in size; an earlier set of barriers is found three-quarters of a whorl further back; the parietal folds of this set have been entirely absorbed, but of the palatal folds there are only three, the second and third horizontal, and the vertical fold; this is shown in fig. 81b *in situ*, while its anterior aspect is given in fig. 81c; the two arrows in fig. 81d indicate the

  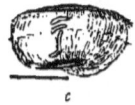

a *b* *c*

Fig. 82.—*Plectopylis achatina* juv.

respective positions of the two sets of barriers. In the McAndrew Collection, University Museum of Zoology, Cambridge, is a tablet with three shells, labelled "*Nanina lacythis*, type, Benson Coll.''; but subsequently altered in pencil to "*P. leiophis (?)*" I refer these specimens without hesitation to immature forms of *Plectopylis achatina*; one of them is shown in figs. 82a-c. This specimen has four and a-half whorls completed, and possesses the immature barriers half a whorl from the aperture. The parietal armature is composed of only a crescent-shaped vertical plate, corresponding to the upper and lower bifurcation of the main horizontal fold (see fig. 82b), while the palatal armature, as it is seen from the outside through the shell-wall, is shown in fig. 82c (enlarged); there are only three folds, *i.e.* the second and third horizontal ones, which are very short and deflected posteriorly, and the vertical fold, with a posterior ridge or support below; the arrow in fig. 82a indicates the position of this set of barriers. The specimen measures 11 : 10 : 6 millimetres respectively; the first three and a-half whorls are ribbed, the last whorl only showing spiral sculpture. The cuticle is plaited transversely, and the whorl is angulated above, at the periphery, and below it; the periphery showing traces of a fringe of laciniae. Below the aperture are found some traces of another set of barriers. The other two specimens referred to measure 9·5 : 8·5 : 5 millimetres; the armature is one-half of a whorl from the aperture, and there are traces of an older set one-quarter of a whorl further back; the upper and the peripherial keels are provided with a fringe of laciniae. These immature specimens are very interesting and instructive, as they tend to indicate the

various stages through which the armatures pass in their evolution from simple to complicated barriers.

Mr. Stoliczka remarks (Journ. Asiat. Soc. Bengal, xl. (1871), p. 221) that *Plectopylis achatina* is "extremely common on all the limestone hills about Moulmain. Among thousands of specimens not one dextrorse variety was met with. The larger specimens I have seen measured in the longer diameter 35 millimetres, but specimens of half that size, and even smaller than that, often have all the appearance of being full-grown." As it is so abundant a species, it is not surprising that it is so frequently seen in collections. It is the most variable of all the species of *Plectopylis*. As none of the many forms has been separated, I venture to name a few of the more prominent varieties.

Plectopylis achatina var. *obesa* ([1]) (figs. 83a-c) is darker in colour above than the type, being of a fuscous chestnut. It is more compressed and distinctly ribbed; the shell is higher in proportion to the diameter, and the umbilicus is deeper; the last whorl does not widen suddenly, and the right margin of the peristome is depressed, the aperture being consequently somewhat ear-shaped; the lower side slopes from the peripherial region to the umbilical angulation. The armature does not

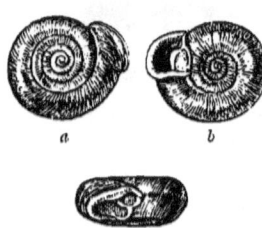

a *b*

c

Fig. 83.—*Plectopylis achatina* var. *obesa.*

differ materially from that of the type, except that the median horizontal parietal fold does not quite reach the apertural ridge. Six specimens were received by me from Miss Linter, five of these being more or less decorticated.

(*To be continued.*)

[Further forms of this species will be described and figured next month.—ED. S.-G.]

([1]) *Plectopylis achatina* var. *obesa*, n. var. (figs. 83a-c), differs from the type in being more compressed and higher in proportion to the diameter; in the last whorl not widening suddenly at the aperture, and in the lower side sloping from the periphery to the umbilical angulation; the right margin of the peristome is depressed; the umbilicus is deeper, and the horizontal median parietal fold does not quite reach the apertural ridge. The shell is darker in colour and more strongly ribbed.—Major diameter, 19 millimetres; minor diameter, 15 millimetres; altitude, 7 millimetres.—Habitat, Moulmain, Burma.—Type in my collection.

ARMATURE OF HELICOID LANDSHELLS

AND NEW FORMS OF PLECTOPYLIS.

By G. K. GUDE, F.Z.S.

(Continued from page 115.)

PLECTOPYLIS achatina var. *infrafasciata* ([1]) (figs. 84*a-c*) is still darker than the variety *obesa*, being of a blackish or purplish-brown. Like that variety it is rounded in contour, but it is larger and more flattened ; while the umbilicus is a little more shallow and the peristome more flattened and reflexed than in the type. The peristome is livid purplish in colour, the left margin being paler and the right margin a little inflected. A whitish or bluish-white band below reaches from the umbilical angulation to the lower suture. The armature is similar to that of the type, but the horizontal parietal fold near the lower suture is visible from the aperture and terminates close to the ridge. The specimen figured was received by me from Mr. Robert Cairns. Four specimens in the collection of Mr. E. L. Layard and one specimen in the McAndrew collection (the latter labelled "*Plectopylis refuga*") all belong to this form. The shell figured in Hanley and Theobald's "Conchologia Indica," t. 57, f. 8 and 9, and Martini und Chemnitz "Conchylien Cabinet" (2) i. t. 66, f. 28-30 (from Mergui, Burma), I also refer to this variety. A specimen measuring 21 millimetres in diameter is in the collection of Mr. Cairns, who also possesses four immature shells.

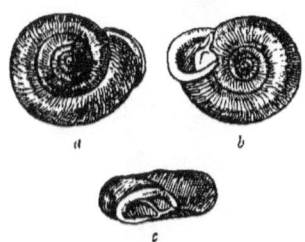

Fig. 84.—*Plectopylis achatina* var. *infrafasciata.*

in various stages of growth, all showing sets of barriers similar to that of the immature *Plectopylis achatina* shown in fig. 81*a*.

([1]) *Plectopylis achatina* var. *infrafasciata*, n. var. (figs. 84 *a-c*), differs from the type in being more rounded in contour, and in the last whorl not widening at the aperture ; the umbilicus is more shallow and the peristome more flattened and reflexed ; the right margin is a little depressed ; the shell is blackish or purplish brown above, with a white or bluish white band below, reaching from the umbilical angulation to the lower suture ; the peristome is purplish brown, the left margin being paler.—Major diameter, 22 millimetres ; minor diameter, 18 millimetres ; altitude, 8 millimetres.—Habitat, Limestone Rocks, Moulmain, Burma.—Type in my collection.

Plectopylis achatina var. *venusta* ([2]) (figs. 85*a-c*) is smaller than any form of *P. achatina* I have seen. It is pale yellowish-white in colour, flammulated with chestnut above and at the sides. It resembles the variety *obesa* in the deeper umbilicus, the sloping underside and in

Fig. 85.—*Plectopylis achatina* var. *venusta.*

the comparative height of the shell ; the median parietal fold does not quite reach the apertural ridge as in that variety, and the lower horizontal parietal fold is not visible from the aperture ; it resembles the type in the sudden widening of the last whorl. The peristome is livid brown, the right margin being a little depressed ; the left margin is paler. The specimen figured was received by me as *Plectopylis pachystoma* Theobald ; but as I am not aware that this name was ever published, and as I have seen other shells so labelled, I consider it expedient to discard the name altogether. A specimen in the collection of Dr. von Möllendorff, likewise labelled *P. pachystoma*, I am unable to separate from the present variety, although it shows no flammulation and the peristome is white ; in other respects it is identical.

Plectopylis achatina var. *castanea* ([3]) (figs. 86*a-c*)

([2]) *Plectopylis achatina* var. *venusta*, n. var. (figs. 85*a-c*), differs from the type and the other varieties in being smaller. It resembles the variety *obesa* in the deeper umbilicus, in the sloping underside, in the comparative height of the shell, and in the median parietal fold not reaching the apertural ridge, but the last whorl widens more, as in the type. In colour it is pale yellowish-white, flammulated with chestnut above and at the side. The peristome is livid brown, the left margin paler, the right margin a little depressed.—Major diameter, 17 millimetres ; minor diameter, 14 millimetres ; altitude, 7 millimetres.—Habitat, Burma.—Type in my collection.

([3]) *Plectopylis achatina* var. *castanea*, n. var. (figs. 86*a-c*), differs from the type in being smaller in diameter and proportionately higher ; it is darker in colour, being blackish-brown above and a little paler below. It resembles the variety *obesa* in being more rounded in outline, in the last whorl not widening suddenly at the aperture, in the sloping underside, and in the median parietal fold not reaching quite to the apertural ridge ; the last two and a half whorls are more strongly decussated above and below than in any other form. An obsolete keel is visible at the periphery.—Major diameter, 21 millimetres ; minor diameter, 19 millimetres ; altitude, 8 millimetres.—Habitat, Burma.—Type in my collection.

is darker than the other forms of *P. achatina*, except the variety *infrafasciata*, being of a blackish-brown above, a little paler below. It is, however, larger than that variety, and does not possess the white band below ; the umbilicus is also much deeper, the shell being in that respect more like the variety *obesa*, which it also resembles in the sloping underside ; the aperture is proportionately larger than in that variety. The spiral lines on

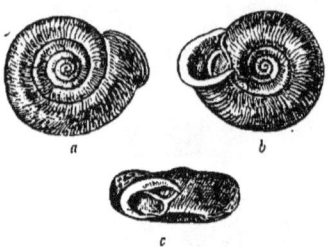

Fig. 86.—*Plectopylis achatina* var. *castanea.*

the last two and a-half whorls are visible without the aid of a lens. The specimen figured was received by me from Miss Linter.

Plectopylis achatina var. *breviplica* ([1]) (figs. 87a-c) has a much shallower umbilicus, and is thinner and more fragile than any other form of *P. achatina* known to me. It is somewhat like the variety *infrafasciata*, but it is devoid of the white band on the lower side ; the last whorl also widens a little more than in that variety, but is less deflected, and the aperture is more sloping from top to base ;

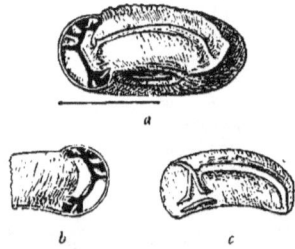

Fig. 87.—*Plectopylis achatina* var. *breviplica.*

there are also important differences in the armature, the lower horizontal parietal fold being very short, not extending on either side beyond the two lower arms of the main fold (see fig. 87c, which shows part of the parietal wall with its folds). Of the palatal armature, the first, second, and third folds are more elevated ; the first is bilobed, and above the posterior portion of the second occurs a very short additional fold. The vertical plate is also more elevated, and in place of the usual denticle posteriorly to its lower extremity is found an elevated ridge quite united to the plate. Fig. 87a shows the anterior and fig. 87b the posterior aspect of both armatures. The specimen figured is in the collection of Mr. Ponsonby.

(*To be continued.*)

([1]) *Plectopylis achatina* var. *breviplica*, n. var. (figs. 87a-c), differs from the type and all the other known varieties by the much more shallow umbilicus. It resembles the variety *infrafasciata* in outline, but it is of a uniform dark brown, with a somewhat polished surface, and the last whorl widens more suddenly at the aperture. The basal horizontal parietal fold is very short, not extending on either side beyond the two lower arms of the main median fold ; the first palatal horizontal fold is considerably more elevated than in the other forms, and is bilobed ; the second and third horizontal folds are also more elevated, the latter fold has a short fold above its posterior portion ; the vertical plate is also more elevated, and in place of the usual denticle posteriorly to its lower extremity is an elevated ridge, quite united to the plate.— Major diameter, 19 millimetres; minor diameter, 16 millimetres; altitude, 7 millimetres.—Habitat, Burma.— Type in Mr. Ponsonby's collection.

ARMATURE OF HELICOID LANDSHELLS

AND NEW FORMS OF PLECTOPYLIS.

BY G. K. GUDE, F.Z.S.

(Continued from page 135.)

PLECTOPYLIS linterae (figs. 88*a-c*), from Pegu, was described by Dr. von Möllendorff in the "Nachrichtsblatt der Deutschen Malakozoologischen Gesellschaft," 1897, p. 28. The shell is sinistral, solid, discoid, widely umbilicated, pale yellow, transversely streaked and flammulated with chestnut, finely and regularly ribbed, smoother below, decussated with microscopic spiral lines. The spire is slightly conical, the apex scarcely produced, and the suture linear. There are six whorls which increase slowly and regularly, and are a little flattened above and rounded below; the last is slightly angulated above the periphery

Fig. 88.—*Plectopylis linterae.*

and around the umbilicus, and descends rather abruptly and deeply in front. The aperture is oblique, heart-shaped. The peristome is white, thickened and strongly reflexed; its margins are united by a strong flexuous raised ridge on the parietal callus. The parietal armature is composed of a slight median horizontal fold, which proceeds from the apertural ridge, is interrupted for a short distance and then continues parallel with the suture for about a quarter of the last whorl; it then gives off a shortly descending, slightly reflexed arm, which is provided anteriorly at the lower extremity with a short horizontal ridge; the fold then rises obliquely for a short distance and finally bifurcates; *the lower arm of the bifurcation is the longer*, and descends obliquely, its lower extremity being provided posteriorly with a short horizontal ridge; the upper arm at first continues to ascend obliquely, then deflects horizontally close to the suture; a short, free, little, horizontal fold occurs below the two lower arms, not extending beyond on either side (see fig. 89*d*, which shows the parietal wall with its folds). The palatal armature consists of: first, a thin long horizontal fold near the suture and parallel with it; secondly, a shorter but stronger broad horizontal fold, which deflects a little and is slightly indented posteriorly; thirdly a still shorter, broad, straight horizontal fold; fourthly, a strong broad vertical plate, which intercalates between the two lower arms of

the parietal fold; this plate is inclined towards the aperture, and its edge is thickened and reflexed; near its lower extremity on the posterior side occurs a strong little denticle, which is elongated horizontally; fifthly, a short thin horizontal fold close to the lower suture, having an elongated denticle a little above its posterior extremity. The species is closely allied to *Plectopylis achatina*, but the spire of the present shell is much more raised, the umbilicus is much deeper, and the whorls more rounded. In the armature this species further differs from *P. achatina* in the median parietal fold being interrupted and much slighter, the branched portion being relatively much more elevated; the lower free horizontal parietal fold is very short, so that this part of the armature, while differing from the typical forms of *P. achatina*, recalls the condition which obtains in the var. *breviplica* of that species. The specimen figured, which I received from Miss Linter, was labelled with the habitat, "Moulmain." It measures: major diameter, 16 millimetres; minor diameter, 13 millimetres; altitude, 6 millimetres.

Plectopylis linterae var. *fusca* (¹) (figs. 89*a-f*). Mr. Ponsonby possesses a shell labelled *P. pachystoma* var. *minor*, which I am unable to separate specifically from *P. linterae*, but which differs from

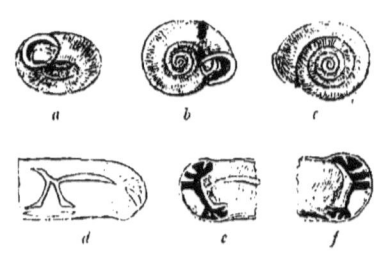

Fig. 89.—*Plectopylis linterae, var. fusca.*

the typical form of that species in being of a unicolorous dark-brown, in the peristome being livid instead of white, and in the shell being thinner in texture. The armatures are identical in both forms. Fig. 89*d* shows the parietal wall with its folds, while fig. 89*e* gives the anterior, and

(¹) *Plectopylis linterae* var. *fusca*, n. var. (figs. 89*a-f*), differs from the type in being unicolorous dark-brown, a little paler below, in being thinner in texture, and in the peristome being livid. Major diameter, 14·5 millimetres; minor diameter, 12·5 millimetres; altitude, 5·5 millimetres.—Habitat, Burma.—Type in Mr. Ponsonby's collection

8*of* the posterior aspect of both armatures; all three figures are enlarged. Figs. 8*9a-c* show the entire shell in three different views, all of natural size.

Plectopylis cairnsi ([2]) (figs. 90*a-g*). I base this new species upon a single unnamed specimen received by me from Mr. Robert Cairns, to whom it was sent

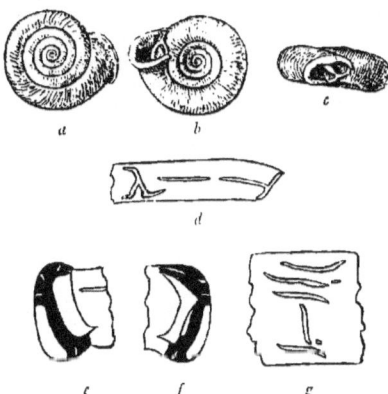

Fig. 90.—*Plectopylis cairnsi.*

by a correspondent in Singapore. Nothing is known of its origin, but the shell, which is somewhat decorticated, appears to have come in contact with red colouring matter, so that it is not improbable it was imported with dye material from Burma, which country, judging from the characters of the shell, may reasonably be supposed to be its native place. At first I was inclined to refer the specimen to *Plectopylis achatina*, but its more rounded contour led me to suspect that it was an un-

(2) *Plectopylis cairnsi*, n. sp. (figs. 90*a-g*), shell sinistrorse, discoid, solid, widely umbilicated, yellowish corneous, finely and regularly ribbed, and decussated with microscopic spiral lines. Spire depressed, apex scarcely prominent, suture distinctly impressed; whorls five and a-half, tumid above, rounded below, increasing slowly and regularly, the last descending moderately in front; aperture oblique, cordate, a little indexed at the upper outer margin. Peristome white, strongly thickened and reflexed; the margins united by a strong raised flexuous ridge on the parietal callus, notched at the junctions above and below. Parietal wall with a strong median fold, given off from the apertural ridge, revolving round about a quarter of the last whorl, but interrupted at the middle; near its posterior extremity occurs a branched fold in the form of the Greek letter λ, *i.e.* an obliquely ascending fold, having anteriorly at its lower extremity a slightly ascending ridge and posteriorly a short support; it is deflexed horizontally at its upper extremity, and at about its middle it gives off an obliquely descending arm, which deflects horizontally at its lower extremity. Palatal folds, five: the first, thin, horizontal, near the suture, a little indented and reflexed opposite the upper extremity of the oblique parietal fold; the second, horizontal, a little shorter and deflexed posteriorly, provided with a small denticle a little above its posterior extremity; the third, still shorter, horizontal, crescent-shaped, its concave side towards the fourth, which is vertical, very strong, inclined towards the aperture; near its lower extremity on the posterior side occurs a minute denticle; the fifth is horizontal, short and very thin.—Major diameter, 18·5 millimetres; minor diameter, 15·5 millimetres; altitude, 6 millimetres.—Habitat, probably Burma.—Type in my collection.

described form, and this suspicion was confirmed on my opening the shell, for I then found the armature to constitute a connecting link between that of the groups of *P. achatina* and *P. ponsonbyi*. I have much pleasure in dedicating this new species to Mr. Cairns, who was kind enough to allow the specimen to pass into my collection. *P. cairnsi* is flatter and more rounded in outline than *P. achatina*; the whorls are more rounded and not angulated, the last whorl widens less at the aperture, the suture is more impressed, the umbilicus less deep, and the peristome is white. The parietal armature differs from that of *P. achatina* and its allies in the median fold being interrupted in the middle and separated from the branched portion which is in the form of the Greek letter λ, and in the total absence of the horizontal fold near the lower suture (see fig. 90*d*, enlarged, which shows the parietal wall with its folds). In the palatal armature there are also some minor differences: the first horizontal fold is indented opposite the upper arm of the branched parietal fold, a feature I have not observed in any other species; the vertical plate is also much narrower than in *P. achatina*, leaving more space for the soft parts of the animal to emerge (see fig. 90*e*, which shows both armatures from the anterior side, and fig. 90*f*, from the posterior side, both enlarged); and, finally, the denticle behind the fifth horizontal fold, present in every other known species of the group of *P. achatina*, is absent (see fig. 90*g*, enlarged, which shows the inside of the outer wall with the palatal armature *in situ*).

Plectopylis (?) *iamcabensis* (figs. 91*a, b*), from Ceylon, was described and figured by Dr. F. Jousseaume in the "Mémoires de la Société Zoologique de France," vii. (1894), p. 278, t. 4, f. 8. As I have

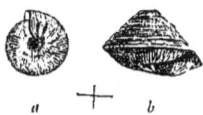

Fig. 91.—*Plectopylis* (?) *iamcabensis* (after Jousseaume).

been unable to obtain a specimen of this species, I have been compelled to rely upon Dr. Jousseaume's description, and to copy his figures of the shell. It is described as follows: shell subperforate, trochiform, stout, somewhat thin, striated and surrounded on the last whorl by three threadlike ridges, diaphanous, shining, corneous white, apex obtuse, suture impressed, crenulate; whorls seven and a-half, flattened, the last angulate, not descending; base more convex, radiately striate; aperture scarcely oblique, subangulate, lunate; peristome simple, straight, columellar margin sloping, near the umbilicus narrowly dilated. Diameter, 4 millimetres; altitude, 3 millimetres. Habitat, Nuwara,

Eliya. No mention whatever is made of any armature, and the systematic position of the

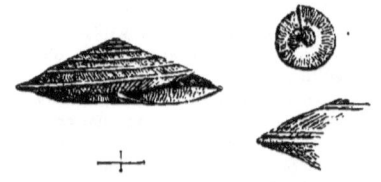

Fig. 92.—*Kaliella* (?) *eugenii* (after Jousseaume).

species, therefore, remains doubtful ; if it really be a *Plectopylis* it will in all probability be found to belong to the section *Sykesia*. Mr. Sykes has doubtfully suggested (Proc. Malac. Soc. London, iii. (1898), p. 71) that it belongs to the genus *Sitala ;* but I do not think this is probable. In the same work (p. 277, t. 4, f. 1) Dr. Jousseaume described another shell which he also places in *Plectopylis, i.e. P. eugenii.* In this case also no mention is made of armature ; moreover, the figure given, which I have copied for convenient reference (see fig. 92), does not at all give the idea of a *Plectopylis,* and I agree with Mr. Sykes in thinking that it may belong to the genus *Kaliella.*

NOTE.—By an oversight fig. 78*f* on page 74 has been placed upside down.

(To be continued.)

ARMATURE OF HELICOID LANDSHELLS
AND A NEW SPECIES OF PLECTOPYLIS.

By G. K. Gude, F.Z.S.

(*Continued from page 172.*)

THREE specimens of an unnamed *Plectopylis* were submitted to me by Messrs. Sowerby and Fulton, who state that they have unfortunately no record of the origin of the shells. Upon examination I found them to belong to an undescribed form, and I have now pleasure in associating with this new species the name of Mr. G. B. Sowerby ([1]). The present shell is closely allied to *Plectopylis plectostoma* and *P. affinis*, a fact which

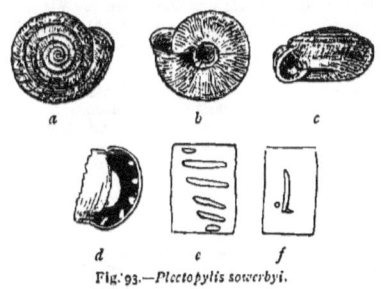

a   *b*   *c*

d   *e*   *f*

Fig. 93.—*Plectopylis sowerbyi.*

led me to re-examine my own specimens of these two species, and among a lot of *P. plectostoma* received from Miss Linter in 1891, labelled "Khasia Hills," I found a decorticated specimen which undoubtedly belongs to the new species.

([1]) *Plectopylis sowerbyi*, n. sp. (fig. 93a-f.).—Shell sinistral, widely umbilicated, discoid, dark corneous, regularly ribbed and radiately distantly plaited, strongly decussated above by spiral ribs, less distinctly so below. Whorls six, narrow, increasing slowly and regularly, somewhat flattened above and rounded below, the last not descending in front. Six or seven spiral ridges, probably, when fresh, bearing rows of hairs, pass round the whole of the body-whorl, the first just above the slightly angular periphery, the others below it. Aperture ear-shaped; peristome slightly tinted with rosy-pink, scarcely thickened, and a little reflexed; the upper outer margin a little depressed; parietal callus slight, without raised ridge at the aperture. Umbilicus deep and wide. The parietal armature consists of a strong vertical plate, provided at its lower extremity with a short support anteriorly, and a small denticle posteriorly. The palatal armature is composed of six more or less horizontal folds, the first very slight and short, near the suture, the four next longer and more elevated, a little deflexed posteriorly, the sixth slight and very short.—Major diameter, 7-9 millimetres; minor diameter, 6·25-7·5 millimetres; altitude, 3·75-4·75 millimetres.—Habitat, Khasia Hills, Assam.—Type in my collection.

P. sowerbyi can at once be distinguished from *P. plectostoma* by the following characters: it is flatter, being less raised in the spire; the umbilicus is more open; there are only six whorls, the last not descending in front; the peristome is scarcely thickened and not much reflexed, and there is no raised ridge on the parietal callus. In the armature there are also important differences: the vertical parietal plate in *P. plectostoma* gives off from its upper extremity anteriorly a horizontal fold, which is absent in *P. sowerbyi*, where the plate in question is only provided with a support anteriorly and a denticle posteriorly below, and there is no horizontal fold below it; so that in this respect the present species differs from both its allies (see fig. 93f, which shows part of the parietal wall with its armature). The palatal armature is in one series, and consists of six horizontal folds. The first fold is very short and slight; the second longest; the third, fourth, and fifth each a little shorter than its predecessor; the sixth slight and very short (see fig. 93e, which shows the inside of the outer wall with its folds). All the figures are enlarged.

In addition to the specimen from the Khasia Hills, mentioned above, I possess an immature shell of unknown origin, which I also refer to *P. sowerbyi*. The last whorl of this specimen is nearly complete, but the armature, which is identical with that of the mature shells, is situate at half a whorl from the aperture.

Plectopylis alphonsi (fig. 94), from the Province

Fig. 94.—*Plectopylis alphonsi.*

of Monpin, Eastern Thibet, was described by Mr. G. P. Deshayes in the "Nouvelles Archives du Museum d'Historie Naturelle de Paris," vi. (1870), p. 22, and figured in the same work, ix. (1873), t. 2, figs. 22-24. The species has not hitherto been referred to the genus *Plectopylis*, but the palatal armature clearly indicates its generic position. Mr. Pilsbry ("Manual of Conchology," ix. p. 211) has placed the species in the genus *Eulota*, but this is doubtless owing to the fact that Mr. Deshayes makes no mention of armature in his diagnosis. Some time ago Mr. Gredler sent me for inspection a single immature specimen from Kouei-Tchou, which he doubtfully referred to the present species. Mr. Mabille, who was kind enough to compare the shell for me with the type of *P. alphonsi* in the Paris Museum, has confirmed its identity with *P. alphonsi*, and subsequently the writer had an opportunity of inspecting the type specimen. Unfortunately there was only one specimen in the museum, so that I was unable to examine the details of the armature. Five horizontal palatal folds are visible through the shell-wall, but probably there are six folds, the first near the suture being seldom visible from without. In general form, as well as in the palatal armature, *P. alphonsi* appears to be allied to *P. stenochila*. The present species was described by Mr. Deshayes as follows:

"Shell depressed, orbiculate-discoid, thin, fragile, corneous-brown, yellowish-white, obliquely lineate and irregularly punctate; spire depressed, scarcely convex; whorls seven, narrow, sub-equal, finely plicate and concentrically sub-striate above; the last angulate above, convex below, polished, widely umbilicated; the perspective umbilicus a little deflected at the aperture; aperture semi-lunate, oblique, slightly compressed; peristome sinuous, reflected; columellar margin wide, with a dentiform thickening.—Major diameter, 9 millimetres; minor diameter, 8 millimetres; altitude, 3·5 millimetres."

Mr. Gredler's specimen, shown in fig 94*a–c*, has the peristome just formed, but is not quite mature. It does not possess any armature, but only shows a few denticles in that part of the shell where the palatal folds would be expected to occur; it has besides some traces of denticles at a spot where a former set of immature barriers might be expected to have existed. This is the first case of a *Plectopylis* without any armature which has come under my observation.

Plectopylis hanleyi was described by Lieut.-Col. Godwin-Austen, in the "Annals and Magazine of Natural History" (5) iv. (1879), p. 164. No figure has been published, and only one specimen is known. This is in the collection of Mr. Sylvanus Hanley, but I have been unable to inspect it, and I am therefore only able to copy the original description. The same remark, unfortunately, applies to the next two species.

The description of *Plectopylis hanleyi* runs thus:

"Shell sinistral, depressedly conoid, openly umbilicated, probably hirsute when young. Sculpture coarse, irregular, transverse ridges. Colour uniform ochraceous. Spire conoidal; apex blunt, smooth. Suture well marked. Whorls six, close-wound, convex; aperture semicircular, diagonal; peristome somewhat thickened, white, with a thin callus on the parietal margin [wall (?)] not to the extent of a ridge. Size.—Major diameter, 5·5; minor diameter, 5; altitude, 3 millimetres.

"Parietal vertical lamina simple; palatal plicae in two rows, four long in front, four short behind, and one basal long.

"This shell is very distinct; it has somewhat the form of *P. plectostoma*, but is not so angular on the periphery, while the internal plication is quite different, besides being so very much smaller in size. Sikkim (?); no history. Only one specimen, in the collection of Mr. Sylvanus Hanley."

Plectopylis vallata was described by Mr. Heude, in the "Journal de Conchyliologie," xxxvii. (1889), p. 45. I translate the description as follows:—

"*Helix vallata.* Shell discoid, laciniate at the periphery; below furnished with acute distant plaits, interspersed with minute striae trellis-like; lat. 10, alt. 5 millimetres. Tchen Keou. This *Plectopylis* recalls *P. stenochila*, but its dimensions are nearly double. Apart from the presence of the peripherial fringe, it may be stated that the inferior plaits are more numerous, and that their intervening spaces are trellised. These characters separate it from its congener of the right bank."

Plectopylis jugatoria was described by Mr. F. C. Ancey in the "Bulletin de la Société Malacologique de France," 1885, p. 127. The diagnosis may be thus translated:—

"Shell widely and deeply umbilicated, depressed, scarcely convex above, apex very prominent, somewhat solid, brownish-red, angulated, the upper oblique lines decussated with spiral ones (except at the apex), produced into laciniate cilia at the periphery; below smoother, spiral lines finer. Whorls six, slowly increasing, separated by a linear suture, almost flattened, the first altogether flat, the last widened around the umbilicus, strongly descending at the aperture, rather acutely angulated above, perspectively convex round the umbilicus below; aperture strongly oblique, not wide; semi-lunate; basal margin regularly rounded, scarcely angled at the periphery; peristome thickened and reflexed all round, but chiefly at the base, whitish; the margins connected by an appressed plate, on both sides at the junctions slightly channelled similar to *Helix achatina* Gray. Palate provided below with five parallel plates with another strong nail-shaped plate opposite the parietal margin; if others exist I have not been able to examine them.

"Major diameter, 12·5–13·25; minor diameter, 11·5–12; altitude, 5·5; width of aperture, 4·5 millimetres. Province of Kouei-Tchou.

"The shell which I have before me is a near relative of *Helix fimbriosa* Martens, of the Provinces Hoo-Nan and Kiang-Si. It can easily be distinguished from that species by the last whorl strongly descending at its extremity, its still more oblique aperture, the fine concentric striae of the lower surface, which is also marked with stronger lines of growth, and especially by the two margins of the aperture being united by a calcareous plate similar to that of the Indian *Plectopylis*, such as *P. achatina, leiophis, cyclaspis, brachyplecta*, etc. At the junction of the two margins exists a little channelled fold as in those species. I believe these internal plates are much like those in *P. fimbriosa*; but the small number of specimens which I had at my disposal did not allow me to sacrifice one to examine the fact completely."

Subsequently Mr. Ancey appears to have modified his view as to the nearest allies of *P. jugatoria*, for he informs me in a letter that this species is allied to *P. laminifera*.

(To be continued.)

ARMATURE OF HELICOID LAND-SHELLS
AND NEW FORMS OF PLECTOPYLIS.
BY G. K. GUDE, F.Z.S.

(Continued from page 2l0.)

Plectopylis giardi (figs. 95a-c.), from Cao-Bang, Tonkin, was described and figured by Dr. H. Fischer in the "Bulletin Scientifique de la France et de la Belgique," xxviii. (1898), p. 320, t. 17, ff. 17-21. The shell is dextrous, very deeply and rather widely umbilicated, brown, finely striated, and decussated with microscopic spiral lines above. The spire is depressed, conical, the apex prominent and the suture distinctly impressed. There are eight whorls, which increase slowly and regularly and are somewhat flattened above and tumid below; the last rounded, obsoletely angulated

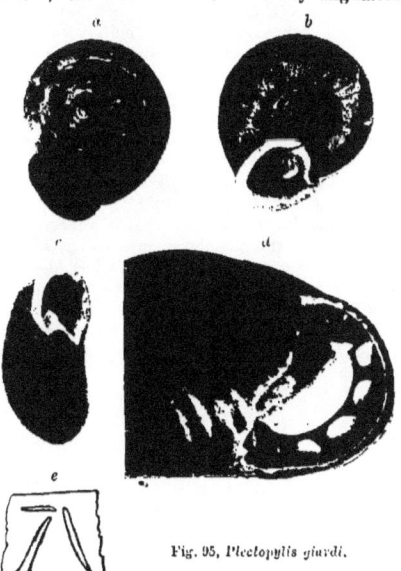

Fig. 95, *Plectopylis giardi.*

above the periphery, descends shortly and suddenly in front. The aperture is oblique, subcircular; the peristome white, rounded, much thickened and strongly reflexed, its margins being united on the parietal callus by a strongly thickened and raised flexuous ridge, which is slightly notched at the junctions above and below. Near the apertural ridge occurs a short but strong oblique fold. (See figs. 95a and c.) The parietal armature consists of two strong obliquely divergent vertical plates, the anterior one shorter, with a slight support on each side at the lower extremity; a short, thin, horizontal fold occurs immediately above it; the posterior one longer, somewhat attenuated at the lower extremity but

rather truncated above. (See fig. 95e, which shows part of the parietal wall with its armature). The palatal armature consists of six short folds: the first thin, horizontal, near the suture; the next four stronger, semicircular, more or less oblique, and intercalated between the two vertical parietal plates; the sixth long and thin. The second of these folds is nearly straight, a little attenuated at both extremities, while the third, fourth, and fifth are almost vertical, reflexed anteriorly above and posteriorly below. *Plectopylis giardi* and the next species are allied to *P. schlumbergeri* figured in this series of papers (vol. iv., 1897, p. 138, f. 58), *P. jovia* (*ibid.*, f. 59), and *P. villedaryi* (*ibid.*, p. 139, f. 60), but can be distinguished at once by the double vertical parietal plate. I am much indebted to Dr. H. Fischer, who kindly allowed me to make use of the photographs of the type shells, which are copied in figs. 95a-d. Figs. 95e and *f* (enlarged) are from a specimen, one of three collected by Dr. Billot, obligingly furnished by Prof. Giard, and now in my collection. This specimen measures: major diameter, 20 millimetres; minor diameter, 17·5 millimetres; altitude, 12 millimetres.

Plectopylis congesta([1]), figs. 96a-*f*. A shell received from Messrs. Sowerby and Fulton as *P. giardi* proved upon examination to differ from that species as well as from all other known forms of

([1]) *Plectopylis congesta*, n. sp. (fig. 96a-*f*).—Shell dextrous, deeply and very widely umbilicated, dark corneous brown, somewhat paler below, finely striated and decussated with microscopic spiral lines which become obsolete below the periphery. Spire depressed, conical; apex prominent; suture slightly impressed. Whorls eight, rounded, increasing slowly and regularly, the last distantly ribbed, suddenly descending somewhat deeply in front; aperture oblique, subcircular. Peristome pale fuscous, thickened and reflexed; the margins united on the parietal callus by a strongly raised flexuous ridge, slightly notched at the junctions above and below. Parietal wall with a strong horizontal entering median fold, running parallel with the suture and united to the apertural ridge. Parietal armature consisting of a strong vertical plate, furnished above and below anteriorly with a slight ridge or support; viewed laterally this plate is seen to be slightly notched at the upper extremity; a second shorter and thinner vertical plate, the lower half of which is obliquely deflexed, occurs behind the first; the lower extremities of the two plates are united by a slight horizontal ridge. Palatal folds six; the first slight, horizontal; the second, third, fourth, and fifth semicircular, oblique; the sixth, horizontal. — Major diameter, 16-18·5 millimetres; minor diameter, 14-15 millimetres; altitude, 9-10 mm.—Habitat, Tonkin.—Type in my collection.

Plectopylis. Its exact locality, unfortunately, was not stated. It differs from *P. giardi* in being smaller, in having a wider umbilicus, in the whorls being less tumid and, as a consequence, the two sets of barriers are in close proximity to each other, so that less space is left for the body of the animal when extended out of the shell. The horizontal fold at the aperture is longer than that of *P. giardi*, and instead of being oblique, as in that species, it is parallel with the suture and is, besides, distinctly united to the apertural ridge. The principal difference, however, lies in the armature, the anterior parietal plate in *P. congesta* being longer than the posterior one,

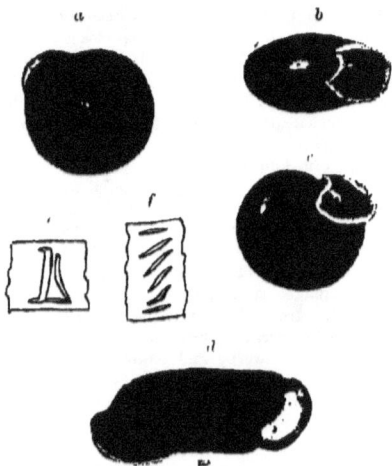

Fig. 96, *Plectopylis congesta.*

whereas the reverse condition obtains in *P. giardi*. Moreover, the horizontal fold above the anterior vertical plate of that species is absent in the present shell, while in its place occurs a horizontal ridge uniting the bases of the two vertical plates. The third, fourth, and fifth palatal folds are oblique instead of being almost vertical, as in *P. giardi*, and nearly straight instead of having their upper and lower extremities bent forwards and backwards respectively. The specimen shown in figs. 96a-c is in Mr. Ponsonby's collection. It measures 18·5:15:10 millimetres, while figs. 96d-f (magnified) are taken from my shell, the dimensions of which are 16:14:9 millimetres.

(²) *Plectopylis achatina* var. *repercussoides,* n. var.—This differs from the type in being angulated above at the periphery, also below round the umbilicus, and in the peristome being white. Armature same as in the type.—Major diameter, 25·27 millimetres; minor diameter, 19·5-22 millimetres; altitude, 8·5-9·5 millimetres.—Habitat Burma.—Type in my collection.

The two foregoing species are connected by an intermediate form of *Plectopylis* still undescribed, but shortly to be published by Dr. Fischer, and which, owing to the kindness of Professor Giard, I was enabled to inspect. This interesting shell combines the characters of the parietal barriers of both the above species, having the two divergent vertical plates and the upper horizontal fold of *P. giardi*, as well as the lower horizontal fold of *P. congesta*. In its palatal armature it differs somewhat from both.

Plectopylis achatina var. *repercussoides* (²). In addition to the new forms described in my previous communications (*ante* pp. 115-133, *et seq.*), I possess a specimen which is intermediate between typical *P. achatina* and *P. repercussa,* having the contour and the white peristome of the latter, but the armature of the former. Thinking it undesirable to base a variety on a solitary shell, it was temporarily placed on one side. Since then Mr. W. E. Collinge has kindly sent me some shells of *Plectopylis* for examination belonging to the museum of Mason's College, Birmingham. Among these I found three specimens which are identical with my shell; all doubts as to its merits to rank as a variety are therefore removed. The variety *repercussoides* differs from the typical *P. achatina* in being angulated above at the periphery, and below round the umbilicus, resembling in this respect *P. repercussa,* with which it has also the white peristome in common. The armature is identical with that of the type. In colour the shell is chestnut brown above, while the umbilical region is white, a feature it shares with the variety *infrafasciata.*

(*To be continued.*)

ARMATURE OF HELICOID LANDSHELLS

AND NEW SPECIES OF PLECTOPYLIS.

By G. K. GUDE, F.Z.S.

(Continued from Vol. V., page 333.)

Plectopylis austeni [1] (figs. 97*a-f*). Four specimens, three adult, one young, of an unnamed form of *Plectopylis*, differing from all described species, have been kindly placed in my hands for examination by Lieut.-Col. Godwin-Austen, with whose name I have much pleasure in associating this new species. The new shell is allied to *Plectopylis oglei* (figured in SCIENCE-GOSSIP, N.S. iv. (1898) p. 263, fig. 68), but it can readily be distinguished from that species by its concave spire; it is also much smaller and much more flattened. In its parietal armature, it differs in having a short and a long median horizontal fold and a denticle in front of the vertical plate, all of which structures are absent in *Plectopylis oglei*. A comparison of the figures will also indicate differences in the palatal armatures of the two species. *Plectopylis austeni* has further some affinity, as regards palatal armature, with *P. muspratti* (c.f.

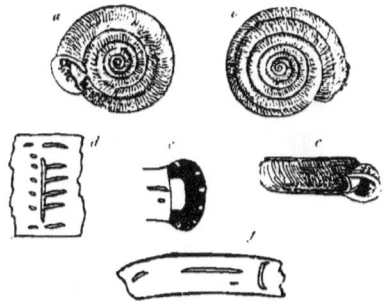

Fig. 97. *Plectopylis austeni.*

SCIENCE-GOSSIP, N.S. iv., 1897, p. 10, f. 45), but the latter is a dextral species and the parietal armature is quite different, as also in the general shape of the shell. The immature specimen of *P. austeni* referred to above has completed five-and-a-half whorls, and is interesting from possessing two sets of armature a quarter of a whorl distant from each other; these differ considerably from the mature barriers; the parietal armature here consists only of the vertical plate and a very short, slight, horizontal fold in front of it. The palatal armature is similar to that of

[1] *Plectopylis austeni*, n.sp. (figs. 97*a-f*). Shell sinistral, discoid, widely umbilicated, ochreous corneous, covered with a deciduous velvety cuticle; finely and closely ribbed, decussated by raised spiral lines, rather distant on the upper side. One of these spiral lines forms a ridge or keel on the upper angle of the whorls above the periphery, revolving above

mature shells, except that the folds, ridge and denticles are very small and slight. Lieut.-Col. Godwin-Austen informs me that the shells were collected by his assistant, Mr. M. T. Ogle, in the Diyung Valley, Singpho, Assam.

Plectopylis woodthorpei [2] (figs. 98 *a-h*). Three specimens—two mature, one young —another undescribed form of *Plectopylis*, have also been most obligingly sent to me for examination by Lieut.-Colonel Godwin-Austen, who informed me that they were collected in 1894 by the late Colonel Woodthorpe, R.E., after whom they are now named. This new species is a very interesting one forming as it does a connecting link between the group of *Plectopylis ponsonbyi* and that of *P. plectostoma*; on the one hand it resembles *P. ponsonbyi* in the posterior portion of the palatal armature (see fig. 98 *f*), and *P. leucochila* in its parietal armature (see fig. 98 *e*); it differs, however, from the other members of this group in having a series of horizontal folds anteriorly to the vertical palatal plate. On the other hand, this biseriate character of the last-mentioned structure, unites it with the group of *P. plectostoma*. In outward appearance the shell of *P. woodthorpei* much

the suture as far as the third whorl. Spire concave, apex a little raised, suture strongly impressed. Whorls 6½, flattened above, rounded below, obsoletely angulated around the umbilicus; increasing slowly at first, the last widening rather suddenly, and descending half the width of the whorl in front; aperture oblique, cordate. Peristome white, strongly thickened and reflexed, the margins united by a strong raised flexuous concave ridge, slightly notched at the junctions above and below. Umbilicus wide and rather shallow. Parietal armature consisting of a short median horizontal fold close to the apertural ridge, and a second longer one farther back, rather elevated posteriorly, gradually descending on the shell wall anteriorly; below its posterior extremity occurs a small denticle; still farther back is found a strong vertical crescent-shaped plate, the upper and lower extremities of which are deflected posteriorly. Palatal armature composed of six short horizontal folds, the first longest, near the suture, provided at its posterior extremity with an elongated denticle; the second, third, fourth, and fifth a little obliquely depressed posteriorly where they are united by a slight vertical ridge, which is continued above the second and below the fifth folds; on the posterior side occur five elongated denticles, the four lower of which correspond to the four folds, while the fifth is situate near the upper extremity of the vertical ridge; the sixth fold is near the lower suture, and has also an elongated denticle posteriorly. — Major diameter, 17·5-19 millimetres; minor diameter, 14·75-16·5 millimetres; altitude, 5·6 millimetres. Habitat, Diyung Valley, Singpho, Assam. Type in the Natural History Museum, South Kensington.

resembles *P. shiroiensis* (*c.f.* SCIENCE-GOSSIP, N.S.
iii., 1896, p. 155, f. 20), but the former is much
larger. The immature specimen referred to, which
has nearly six whorls formed, has the armature incomplete, and is instructive as possibly throwing
some light upon the evolution of these structures.
The parietal armature here possesses the two vertical
plates, but the horizontal folds given off by the
anterior plate are very short, being only one quarter
of the length of those in the mature shells; the thin
fold near the lower suture is not compressed into a
lamellar fold below the vertical plates, as is the case
in the full-grown shells, and it rises much farther
back (see fig. 98 *g*, which shows portion of the
parietal wall with its armature. Of the palatal
armature, only the posterior series of pro-

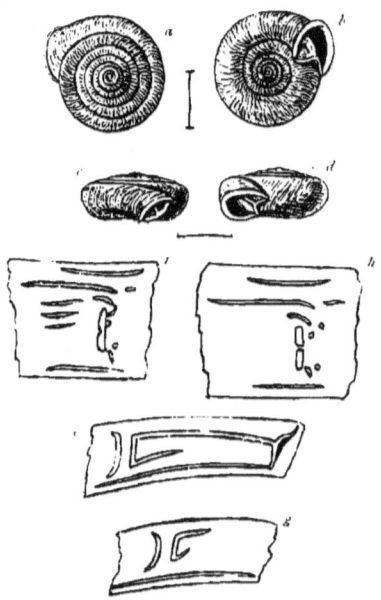

Fig. 98.—*Plectopylis woodthorpei.*

cesses is present, the anterior series having
still to be formed: a fact clearly pointing
to the more recent origin of the biseriate forms.
The vertical plate is distinctly divided into two sub-
equal portions, in consequence of the indentation in
the middle being carried down to the base: the ridge
connecting the upper extremity of the vertical plate
with the short horizontal fold above it is absent, but
in its stead occurs near the latter a little denticle;
while posteriorly to the upper half of the vertical
plate is found a distinct denticle, corresponding to
the slight swelling in the same place, mentioned in
the diagnosis (see fig. 98 *h*, which shows the inside
of the palatal wall with its armature).

Plectopylis (*Sykesia*) *biciliata* (figs. 99 *a-c*) from
Ceylon was described by Dr. Pfeiffer in the "Pro-
ceedings of the Zoological Society," 1855, p. 112, as
Helix biciliata, and the shell is figured in "Hanley
and Theobald's Conchologia Indica" (1875), t. 159,
figs. 1 and 4. The systematic position of this shell
remained uncertain for a long time: it was placed in
Nanina by Dr. Pfeiffer ("Malak. Blätter" ii., 1855,
p. 121), and in *Discus*, by Mr. H. Nevill ("Enum.
Helic. Ceylan." 1871, p. 1), while finally Mr. S.
Clessin grouped it with *Macrochlamys* ("Nomencl.
Helic. viv." 1881, p. 45). It is unfortunate that
Dr. Pfeiffer's types of this species cannot be found.
They were described as from the late Major Skinner's
collection, but Miss Linter who purchased the entire
collection, kindly informs me that the shells in
question are not in it, and she does not think that
Major Skinner ever possessed them there being no
record of them in his catalogues. Mr. Edgar Smith

(²) *Plectopylis woodthorpei*, n. sp. (figs. 98 *a-h*).—
Shell dextral, discoid, widely and deeply umbilicated,
dark corneous, finely and regularly ribbed, closely
decussated by microscopic spiral lines. Spire conical,
apex prominent, suture impressed. Whorls 6½, increasing slowly and regularly. flattened above, tumid
below, the last scarcely wider than the penultimate,
bluntly keeled above the periphery, widening a little
towards the aperture, descending deeply in front.
Aperture oblique, cordate; peristome whitish,
strongly thickened and reflexed, the margins united
by a strongly raised flexuous ridge, which is concave
in the middle, and notched at the junctions above and
below. Parietal armature consisting of two nearly
parallel vertical plates, the posterior one longer,
slightly reflexed posteriorly at its lower extremity,
and provided posteriorly at the upper extremity with
a slight ridge: the anterior one shorter, giving off a
horizontal fold anteriorly at each extremity, the
lower less than half the length of the upper, ascending obliquely: the upper revolving almost parallel with
the suture, following the deflexion of the whorl, and
joining the ridge at the aperture. Below the posterior
vertical plate rises a free, thin, horizontal fold, at
first considerably elevated above the shell-wall, but
suddenly becoming attenuated and threadlike, running parallel with the lower suture, as far as the
aperture where it is joined to the ridge on the parietal
callus. Palatal armature in two series, the posterior
series consisting of: first, a long thin horizontal
fold near the suture; secondly, a very long horizontal fold, extending anteriorly beyond the
folds of the second series, with an elevated
compressed denticle posteriorly; thirdly, a very
short horizontal fold, deflexed posteriorly;
fourthly, a strong vertical plate, with an indentation at the middle, giving off posteriorly at its
lower extremity an obliquely descending ridge, and
provided at the same place with a small denticle: at
the base of the upper lobe of the vertical plate on the
posterior side occurs a slight swelling, while on the
same side from its upper extremity runs a short ridge,
connecting this plate with the third horizontal fold:
fifthly, a long thin horizontal fold near the lower
suture. The anterior series consists of three thin
horizontal folds, the first longest the third shortest,
all three descending a little anteriorly.—Major diameter, 8·75-10 millimetres, minor diameter, 7·25-8
millimetres, altitude 3·25-4 millimetres.—Habitat,
Fort Stedman, Burma.—Type in the British Museum.

has obligingly searched the British Museum collection for these types, but without success. The species appears to be rare, for since it was first described, it has remained unobserved until Mr. H. B. Preston found a single specimen at Patapolla, Ceylon, as recorded by Mr. E. R. Sykes ("Proc. Malac. Soc., London," iii., 1898, p. 66), and Mr. O. Collett subsequently found two

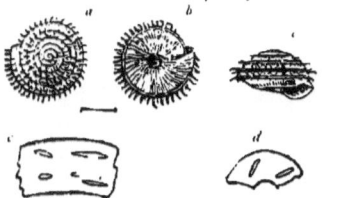

Fig. 99. *Plectopylis biciliata.*

specimens at Haputale (Sykes, op. cit. p. 160). The three specimens referred to agree with the figures in "Conchologia Indica," and it may, therefore, be safely assumed that they are correctly identified, and to Mr. Sykes belongs the credit of first pointing out the true systematic position of the species. The shell is convexly conical, narrowly umbilicated, dark corneous, translucent, finely and regularly ribbed, with a double keel at the periphery and a third a little above it, the lowest and uppermost being provided with a fringe of coarse, curved, deciduous hairs. There are six convex whorls, which increase slowly and regularly, the base a little shining, tumid around the narrow umbilicus and concave towards the periphery. The aperture is subquadrate, elongated, the peristome simple, acute. The parietal armature consists of two simple obliquely ascending folds, separated by a distance of half a whorl, having the upper extremities somewhat attenuated and the lower truncate. (See fig. 99*d*, which shows the parietal wall with its two folds). The palatal armature is composed of : first, a short, horizontal fold below the periphery, a little farther back but in a line with it a strong lamelliform denticle, ascending obliquely ; secondly, three denticles in a line horizontally and about equidistant, the posterior one strongest ; thirdly, a short slight horizontal fold near the lower suture, rising near the aperture and revolving as far as the second denticle. (See fig. 99*c*, which shows the inside of the outer wall with the palatal armature). The specimen shown in figs 99*a-c* measures 6 millimetres in diameter, altitude 3·5 millimetres ; it is one of the shells collected by Mr. Collett and is in Mr. Ponsonby's collection : the armatures are figured from the specimen collected by Mr. Preston which is in Mr. Sykes' collection.

(*To be continued.*)

ARMATURE OF HELICOID LANDSHELLS

AND NEW SPECIES OF PLECTOPYLIS.

By G. K. GUDE, F.Z.S.

Rec'd Feb. 14/00

(Continued from page 47.)

Plectopylis (Sykesia) caliginosa (figs. 100*a-e*) from Ambagamuwa, Ceylon, was described and figured by Mr. Sykes, in the "Proceedings of the Malacological Society of London," iii. (1898), p. 72, t. 5, ff. 21, 22. The shell is lenticular, narrowly umbilicated, ochreous corneous, opaque, very finely and regularly ribbed, the ribs being rather more prominent above than below; it is acutely keeled at the periphery, with a raised spiral line above the keel, quite close to it, as far as the apical whorl. The spire is conical, the apex obtuse, the suture impressed. There are five very slowly increasing whorls, flattened above, tumid below, the last scarcely wider than the penultimate, not descending in front. The aperture is almost vertical, lunate, and the peristome simple, acute. The parietal armature consists of two simple, sub-vertical plates which are somewhat thickened and truncate at the lower, and attenuated at the upper extremities; these plates are separated by a distance of a quarter of a whorl, and the posterior one is the stronger (see

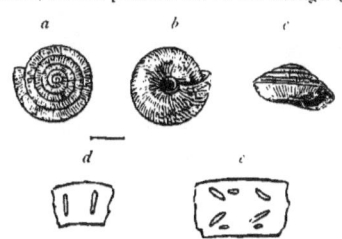

Fig. 100.—*Plectopylis caliginosa.*

fig. 100*d*, which shows the parietal wall with its two plates). The palatal armature is in two vertical series: the anterior series consists of an obliquely ascending short quadrate tooth near the periphery, and below this an obliquely descending lamelliform tooth, with a slight, horizontally elongated denticle below its posterior extremity; the posterior series is similar to the anterior one, but the teeth are stronger and thicker in the former, while there is in addition a horizontally elongated denticle on the anterior side of the upper tooth. The specimen shown in figs. 100*a-e* measures 6 millimetres in diameter, alt. 3 millimetres, and is in the collection of Mr. Ponsonby. The armatures are figured from the type specimen in the collection of Mr. Sykes, who kindly permitted me to open the shell for the examination of the armature.

Plectopylis (Sykesia) clathratula, var. *compressa*, (figs. 101*a-c*) was described and figured by Mr. Sykes, in the "Proceedings of the Malacological Society," iii. (1898), p. 72, t. 5, ff. 13, 14. It

differs from the type in being more elevated, in the more convex spire and the narrower umbilicus, while the raised ribs are scarcely visible. The armature is

Fig. 101. *Plectopylis clathratula* var. *compressa.*

similar to that of the type. The specimen figured is in Mr. Ponsonby's collection; it measures 5 millimetres in diameter, altitude 2·5 millimetres.

Plectopylis françoisi (figs. 102*a-e*) from Déo-ma-Phuc, Tonkin, was described and figured by Dr. H. Fischer, in the "Journal de Conchyliologie, xlvi. (1898), pp. 214-218, ff. 1, 3, 4 (part published March, 1899). The shell is dextral, deeply and widely umbilicated, corneous, striated, and decussated with microscopic spiral lines above, which become obsolete at the periphery, the lower surface smooth and a little shining. The spire is depressed, conical, the apex prominent and the suture distinctly impressed. There are 7½ whorls, which increase slowly and regularly, and are somewhat flattened above and tumid below. The last whorl is at first obsoletely keeled above the periphery and angulated at the umbilical region near the parietal callus; it descends shortly and suddenly in front. The aperture is a little oblique, subcircular; the peristome white, a little thickened and reflexed, its margins united by a parietal callus. The parietal armature is composed of two strong, obliquely divergent, transverse plates, the anterior one shorter, rounded at the upper and giving off an anterior ridge at the lower extremity; a short thin horizontal fold occurs immediately above it; the posterior plate longer, truncate at the upper, attenuated at the lower extremity. A free thin horizontal fold occurs below these plates, terminating on the one side just below the anterior plate, and on the other just in front of the posterior plate. (See fig. 102*d*, which shows part of the parietal wall with its armature). The palatal armature consists of six folds: the first, rather short, thin, horizontal, near the suture; the second longest of all, horizontal, deflected at the posterior extremity and becoming slowly attenuated anteriorly; the third, fourth, and fifth stronger, semicircular, oblique, their anterior extremities a little reflexed, their posterior ones a little deflexed; the sixth thin, long, horizontal; the second, third, fourth, and fifth give off, about the middle, from the lower side, a slight callous ridge which connects them *inter se*; between the posterior extremities of the fifth and

D 4

sixth folds is a horizontally elongated denticle. (See fig. 102c, which shows the inside of the outer wall with the palatal folds, and fig. 102c, which gives the anterior view of both armatures). *Plectopylis françoisi* is intermediate as regards its armature between *P. giardi* and *P. congesta*, as already briefly stated when describing the latter species (SCIENCE-GOSSIP N.S. v., p. 333); *P. françoisi* differs from *P. giardi*, 1° in the anterior parietal plate being more oblique, and 2° in this plate being rounded at the upper extremity instead of truncated; 3° in having an additional free horizontal parietal fold; 4° in the second and sixth palatal folds being longer; 5° in the second, third, fourth, and fifth palatal folds being more oblique, and 6° in having in addition a denticle between the fifth and sixth folds; 7° in the armature being further from the aperture, 8° in the aperture being less oblique,

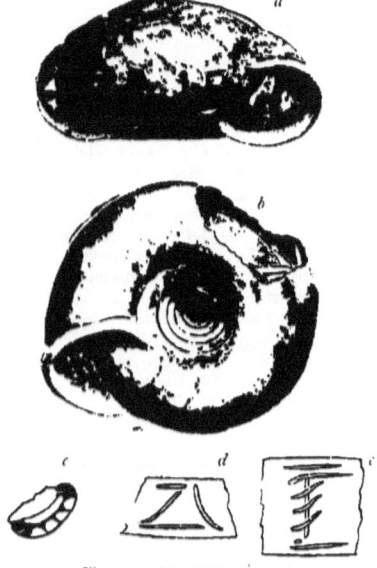

Fig. 102.—*Plectopylis françoisi.*

and 9° in the peristome being considerably less thickened and reflexed. The shell is, moreover, considerably smaller, and the sculpture much stronger. From *P. congesta* it differs similarly in the characters enumerated under Nos. 3, 4, 6, 8, and 9; while in the character of the anterior parietal plate it is still further removed, this structure in *P. congesta* is almost vertical, and it wants the upper free horizontal parietal fold, while the lower horizontal fold is joined to the two transverse plates. The unique specimen is in the collection of Professor Giard, who obligingly sent it to me for examination; it is, unfortunately, slightly damaged, that portion of the parietal callus which bears the short fold near the aperture in the other species, together with the ridge,

being broken off, so that it is impossible to say whether the present species differs from its two congeners in this respect. The shell measures major diameter 15.5 millimetres, minor diameter 13.5 millimetres, altitude 8.75 millimetres. Figs. 102a-b are taken from photographs kindly furnished by Dr. H. Fischer.

Plectopylis revoluta was described by Dr. Pfeiffer in the "Malakozoologische Blätter," xiv. (1867), p. 64, as from the Andaman Islands. Unfortunately, I have been unsuccessful in tracing the whereabouts of the specimens from which the diagnosis was drawn up, as Mr. Smith, who kindly searched the collection in the British Museum, has been unable to find them there; and Professor Boettger informs me that they are not in the Pfeiffer collection acquired by Dr. Dohrn. This is all the more to be regretted as no *Plectopylis* has since been discovered in the Andaman Islands. The late Mr. Stoliczka ("Journ. Asiat. Soc. Bengal," xl. (1871), p. 223) was of opinion that this shell could hardly be distinct from *Plectopylis cyclaspis*, his specimens of which agreed perfectly with the measurements given by Dr. Pfeiffer. He adds that amongst many thousands of shells from the Andaman Islands, he never received *cyclaspis*, and he doubted its occurrence there as much as that of *P. achatina*, recorded by Tryon in "Proc. Asiat. Soc.," 1870, p. 88. It is advisable, I think, to consider *P. revoluta* synonymous with *P. cyclaspis*.

ADDENDA.

Plectopylis giardi (fig. 103).—I append a figure showing the inside of the outer wall of *P. giardi*, with

Fig. 103.—*Plectopylis giardi* (Palatal folds).

its palatal folds. This figure, by an oversight, was omitted when the species was described and figured (SCIENCE-GOSSIP, N.S. v., p. 332, fig. 95).

Plectopylis feddeni (figs. 104a and b).—When considering this species (SCIENCE-GOSSIP, iv., p. 171, fig. 64) I had not seen any specimen, and was obliged to copy Lieut.-Colonel Godwin-Austen's description and figures, in which no indication is given of the palatal armature. Mr. W. T. Blanford has oblig-

Fig. 104.—*Plectopylis feddeni.*

ingly allowed me to examine the type specimens which are in his collection, and I am now able to supplement the figures already published with a view of the palatal armature and one of the parietal armature of an immature shell. The shell of which the parietal armature was figured has the outer wall of the last whorl broken away ; in a second specimen—not quite mature—this portion of the outer wall is also missing ; the upper horizontal fold in the latter specimen is very short, and the third (anterior) transverse fold has not been formed (see fig. 104*b*). A third specimen is entire ; but, as the shell is somewhat translucent, I was enabled by wetting it to make out the conformation of its palatal armature without much difficulty, and the figure I have given of it represents these structures as they would appear if looked at from the inner side (see fig. 104*a*). It will be seen that the first (upper) fold is almost horizontal : the second is longer, a little deflected posteriorly, where it is also attenuated, but truncated anteriorly : the third is shorter, oblique, curved ; the fourth sub-vertical, bilobed at its middle, and furnished on the posterior side with two small denticles, one near its middle, and one near its lower extremity : the fifth is sub-horizontal, and has its two extremities a little deflected ; a little denticle occurs near its posterior extremity. From these features, hitherto unrecorded, it will be seen that this species belongs to the group of *P. ponsonbyi*, its nearest ally being *P. leucochila* (SCIENCE-GOSSIP, iv., p. 231, fig. 66). Since the foregoing remarks were written, I have been so fortunate as to acquire a specimen of *P. feddeni*, appar-

ently communicated by Mr. Hungerford to Mr. Langdon. This specimen, also, has only two transverse parietal folds, so that it is somewhat uncertain whether the third (anterior) transverse fold is of any diagnostic value.

Plectopylis shanensis (fig. 105.) (See SCIENCE-GOSSIP, iv., p. 36, fig. 48). I append a figure acci-

Fig. 105.—*Plectopylis shanensis*.

dentally omitted, giving a view of the shell, with part of the outer wall removed, exposing the parietal armature.

Mr. Ponsonby has drawn my attention to an erroneous statement on page 17, with regard to his specimen of *P. bicilliata* which, he informs me, was not collected by Mr. Collett, but came from the Morelet Collection, labelled as from Neville.

All known forms of *Plectopylis* have now been considered ; and I propose to conclude this series of papers with a synopsis, a key to the species, a map showing their geographical distribution, and a general index.

(*To be continued.*)

ARMATURE OF HELICOID LANDSHELLS

AND

NEW SECTIONS OF PLECTOPYLIS.

By G. K. GUDE, F.Z.S.

(*Continued from p. 77.*)

THE genus *Plectopylis* was established by Mr. Benson in the "Annals and Magazine of Natural History" (3), v., (1860), p. 244, and in the preceding volume of the same publication (3), iv., (1859), p. 95, he described the external characters of the animal of *P. achatina*. Mr. Stoliczka, however, was the first to examine some species anatomically (Journ. Asiat. Soc. Bengal, 1871, p. 217), the forms investigated by him being *P. achatina*, *P. cyclaspis*, *P. pinacis*, and *P. macromphalus*. He states that on the whole form of the body closely resembles that of *Clausilia*, and that a comparison of the interior organisation of the two genera also indicates their close relation. On comparing the jaw of *Plectopylis* with that of *Clausilia*, he found both similar in structure, but the shape different and the transverse sulcation only indicated in the latter genus. Much greater, he continues, is the similarity of the *Plectopylis* jaw with that of *Cylindrella*, with the exception that the median projection is wanting in the *Cylindrella* jaw. The arrangement of the teeth of *P. achatina* and *P. cyclaspis* he also found to agree with that of *Cylindrella* in the very small size of the centre tooth, but this was not found to be a constant character. In *P. pinacis* the centre tooth was larger and more of a shape similar to that of the lateral teeth, which, however, in all the species he found to retain distinctly the helicoid character.

The true systematic position of *Plectopylis* still seems uncertain. Mr. Pilsbry doubtfully places it in the family Helicidae between the groups Macroogona and Teleophallogona (Manual of Conch. ix., Index to the Helicidae, 1895, p. 124). He includes two Chinese groups of uncertain affinities, Traumatophora

and Stegodera, each containing one species, but as nothing is known of their anatomy, and as, moreover, they are devoid of the armature characteristic of *Plectopylis*, I consider it expedient, for the present, to exclude them.

The shells of *Plectopylis* are characterised by a more or less depressed discoid form, with a flat or conical spire and a large open umbilicus (narrow in the section Sykesia), the upper surface is usually sculptured with spiral lines, and the immature shells are hirsute. The aperture is semi-circular or lunate, the peristome somewhat expanded and generally thickened, its ends usually united by an elevated ridge on the parietal callus, which has often an entering fold. The armature consists of a vertical or transverse plate or plates with accessory horizontal or oblique folds on the parietal wall; and transverse, horizontal or oblique folds and denticles on the palatal wall. "When the animal retracts into its shell, the passage through the folds is generally found to be filled up with mucous secretion, but the body itself mostly retracts one-half of a whorl further inwards. During hibernation the aperture is besides closed with the usual calcareous lamina, as in the other *Helicidae*." (Stoliczka, 'Journ. Asiat. Soc. Bengal, 1871, p. 218).

Mr. Benson noted that *Plectopylis achatina* was ovo-viviparous, and this was found to be the case with all the species examined by Mr. Stoliczka. One specimen of *P. cyclaspis* he found to contain three well-developed embryos, each consisting of three convolutions, regularly coiled in and enclosed in a thin soft sac of calcareous granules, loosely joined together. I have also observed this fact in a specimen of *P. lissochlamys* in Mr. Fulton's possession.

Mr. Benson divided the genus into three sections; the typical section comprising *P. achatina* and *P. cyclaspis*; the second section consisting of *P. refuga* and *P. leiophis*, while the third section contained *P. plectostoma* and *P. pinacis*. The great number of species discovered since Benson's time necessitates still further division, and I propose the following synopsis.

I. Section ENDOTHYRA, n. sec. Type *P. plecto-stoma*. (Third section of Benson). Sinistral. Umbilicus moderate. Palatal folds horizontal or oblique.

Habitat : Sikkim, Assam, Burma.

1. P. minor, G.A.　Darjeeling, Sikkim ; Naga Hills, Assam.
2. P. hanleyi, G.A.　Sikkim.
3. P. blanda, Gude.　Naga Hills.
4. P. macromphalus, W. Blf.　Darjeeling ; Khasia Dafla and Naga Hills.
5. P. sowerbyi, Gude.　Khasia Hills.
6. P. plectostoma, Bens.　Darjeeling, Sikkim ; Dafla Khasia and Naga Hills, Sylhet, Kohima, Assam ;　Cherra Poonjee, Munipur ;　Bassein, Arakan. Pegu.
　　　prodigium, Bens.
　　　v. tricarinata, Gude.　Khasia Hills.
7. P. affinis, Gude.　Khasia Hills.
8. P. pinacis, Bens. Darjeeling, Bungmaval, Sikkim.
　　　pettos, Mts.
9. P. fultoni, G.A.　Khasia Hills.

II. Section CHERSAECEA, n. sec. Type *P. leiophis*. (Second section of Benson).　Sinistral or dextral. Umbilicus wide.　Palatal folds horizontal or oblique. Sometimes with one oblique or vertical plate.

Habitat : from Assam through Upper Burma and Laos to Tenasserim.

10. P. muspratti, Gude.　Naga Hills, Assam.
11. P. austeni, Gude.　Diyung Valley, Singpho, Assam.
12. P. oglei, G.A.　Sadiya, Assam.
13. P. serica, G.A.　Naga Hills.　North Cachar.
　　　sericata, Hanley and Theob.
14. P. munipurensis, G.A.　Munipur.　N.E. Frontier, Bengal.
15. P. nagaensis, G.A.　Naga Hills.
16. P. pseudophis, W. Blf.　Thayet Myo, Pegu.
17. P. leiophis, Bens.　Thayet-Myo, Kivadouk, Akou oung, Pegu.
　　　refuga, auct.
18. P. refuga, Gould.　Tavoy, Tenasserim. Pegu.
19. P. perrierae, Gude.　Thayet-Myo, Pegu.
20. P. shiroiensis, G. A.　Shiroifurar, Munipur.
21. P. perareta, W. Blf.　Mya Leit Doung. Ava. Haindet, Upper Burma.
22. P. brachydiscus, G. A.　Moulmain, Tenasserim.
23. P. dextrorsa, G. A.　Tenasserim.
24. P. shanensis, Stol.　Pegu ; Shan states.
　　　trilamellaris, G. A.
25. P. brahma, G. A. Brahmakhund, E. Assam.
26. P. andersoni, W. Blf.　Bhamo, Ava, Upper Burma.　Hoetone, Yunnan.
27. P. iaomontana, Pfr.　Luang Prabang, Laos.

III. Section ENDOPLON, n. sec.　Type *P. brachyplecta*.　Dextral.　Palatal folds horizontal, oblique, or almost vertical.

Habitat : Tonkin, Burma.

28. P. smithiana, Gude.　Attaram, Burma.
29. P. brachyplecta, Bens.　Moulmain.
30. P. giardi, H. Fischer.　Cao-Bang, Tonkin.
31. P. congesta, Gude.　Tonkin.
32. P. françoisi, H. Fischer. Deo-Ma-Phuc, Tonkin.
33. P. jovia, Mab.　Halong, Tonkin.
34. P. schlumbergeri, Morlet.　Halong, Elephant Mountain, Nuy-Dong-Nay, Tonkin.
35. P. villedaryi, Ancey.　Lang-Son, Bac-Ninh, Tonkin.
36. P. phlyaria, Mab.　Tonkin.

IV. Section PLECTOPYLIS, s. s.　Type *P. achatina*. (Typical section of Benson).　Sinistral.　Shell flattened.　Palatal armature : one vertical plate with three horizontal folds above, one below.

Habitat : Burma.

37. P. ponsonbyi, G.A.　Haindet, Burma.
38. P. lissochlamys, Gude.　Moulmain.
39. P. magna, Gude.　Moulmain. Taunghu, Pegu.
40. P. woodthorpei, Gude.　Fort Stedman, Burma.
41. P. leucochila, Gude.　Burma.
42. P. feddeni, W. Blf.　Prome, Pegu.
43. P. cairnsi, Gude.　Burma.
44. P. cyclaspis, Bens.　Moulmain ; Tenasserim.
　　　catinus, Bens.
　　　revoluta, Pfr.
45. P. karenorum, W. Blf.　Arakan Hills ; Henzada ; Pegu.
　　　burmanica, Bens, M.S.
46. P. linterae, Mlldff.　Pegu.
　　　v. fusca, Gude.
47. P. anguina, Gld.　Tavoy, Tenasserim.
48. P. achatina, Gray.　Moulmain ; Tavoy.
　　　v. repercussoides, Gude.　Burma.
　　　v. infrafasciata, Gude.　Moulmain.
　　　v. castanea, Gude.　Burma.
　　　v. obesa, Gude.　Moulmain.
　　　v. venusta, Gude.　Burma.
　　　pachystoma, Theob. M.S.
　　　v. breviplica, Gude.　Burma.
49. P. repercussa, Gld.　Moulmain. Tavoy.

V. Section SINICOLA, n. sec.　Type *P. fimbriosa*. Dextral.　Palatal folds horizontal.

Habitat : China ; Tibet 1 species.

50. P. emoriens, Gredl.　Hoo-Nan.
51. P. azona, Gredl.　Badung, Hoo-Pé.
52. P. pulvinaris, Gld.　Canton ; Hongkong.
53. P. fimbriosa, Mts.　Kiang-Si.
　　　v. nana, Mlldff.
　　　v. continentalis, Mlldff.
54. P. reserata, Heude.　Tchen-Keou.　Badung Hoo-Pé.
55. P. laminifera, Mlldff.　Hoo-Pé.
56. P. jugatoria, Anc.　Kouei-Tchou.
57. P. diptychia, Mlldff.　Kouei-Tchou.
58. P. biforis, Heude.　Ta-Kouan-Tchen.
59. P. stenochila, Mlldff.　Hoo-Pé.
　　　v. basilia, Gude.　Badung, Hoo-Pé.

60. P. alphonsi, Desh. Moupin, E. Tibet.
61. P. murata, Heude. Tchen-Keou.
62. P. cutisculpta, Mlldff. Fud-Shien.
63. P. invia, Heude. Tchen-Keou.
64. P. secura, Heude. Kouang-Si.
65. P. multispira, Mlldff. Hoo-Nan.
66. P. schistoptychia, Mlldff. Hoo-Nan.
67. P. vallata, Heude. Tchen-Keou.
VI. Section ENTEROPLAX, n. sec. Type *P. quadrasi*. Dextral.
Habitat : Philippine Islands.
68. P. quadrasi, Mlldff. Cebu : Siquior.
    v. boholensis, Gude. Bohol.
69. P. quadrasi, Mlldff. Luzon.
70. P. polyptyehia, Mlldff. Cebu.

VII. Section SYKESIA, Gude (1897), SCIENCE-GOSSIP, N.S. iii., p. 332. AUSTENIA, Gude *ib.*, p. 300, pre-occupied by Nevell (1878). Type, *P. clathratula*. Dextral, shell translucent, acutely keeled.
Habitat : Southern India. Ceylon.
71. P. retifera, Pfr. Nilgiri and Shevroi Hills, So. India.
72. P. clathratuloides, Gude. Anarmalai Hills. So. India.
73. P. clathratula, Pfr. Ceylon.
    putcolus, Bens.
    putcolus, Bens.
    v. compressa, Sykes. Ceylon.
74. P. caliginosa, Sykes. Ceylon.
75. P. biciliata, Pfr. Ceylon.

I strongly suspect that when the anatomy of the Philippine species (Section Enteroplax) is investigated the group will be found to differ so widely from typical *Plectopylis* that it will have to be raised to the rank of a separate genus. The same may prove to be the case with the section Sykesia. It is somewhat difficult to hazard an opinion as to the primordial form from which the present species of Plectopylis have been evolved as no fossil forms are known, and likewise it is almost impossible to judge as to which of the known forms are the most archaic, for the armatures of immature specimens, as far as they have come under my observation, throw no light on the subject, as they did in the case of Corilla (c.f. SCIENCE-GOSSIP, N.S. iii., 1896, p. 128) ; except in size and in the lengths of the folds, the barriers of mature and immature shells of Plectopylis, are almost identical. There is one exception in this respect, i.e., *Plectopylis woodthorpei*, in which, as I pointed out (*ante* p. 16), the palatal folds of the anterior series are only found in mature shells. It may, however, be assumed that the simple armatures preceded the more complicated, and on this assumption *P. achatina* and its allies, with their complex parietal barriers, must be regarded as the most recent : while in another direction, *P. plectostoma* and its congeners, with their biserial palatal folds, have presumably been evolved from some monoserial predecessor, of which *P. sowerbyi* may be taken as a less modified representative.

(To be concluded.)

Rec'd Feb 14/00

ARMATURE OF HELICOID LANDSHELLS.

By G. K. GUDE, F.Z.S.

(Concluded from page 149.)

WITH regard to the geographical distribution, as far as our present knowledge enables us to judge, the genus is confined to Sikkim, Assam, Further India and China, extending south to Tenasserim, north as far as Central China, west to Sikkim, and east to Tonkin, with two outlying groups : one in the southern extremity of the Indian Peninsula and Ceylon, the other in the Philippine Islands.

On looking at the accompanying map, where I have indicated all the known species at their respective believe, who has traversed this region, informs me he collected forms of *Plectopyli* there, but I have not yet been able to inspect them. Crossing the Himalayan Range we find one species in Eastern Tibet, *P. alphonsi*, while China, including Hongkong, has no less than seventeen species. A wide gap separates the Sikkim forms from the South Indian and the Cingalese species, a fact which will be less surprising, if, as I suspect, the latter prove to belong to a distinct genus. In all probability further

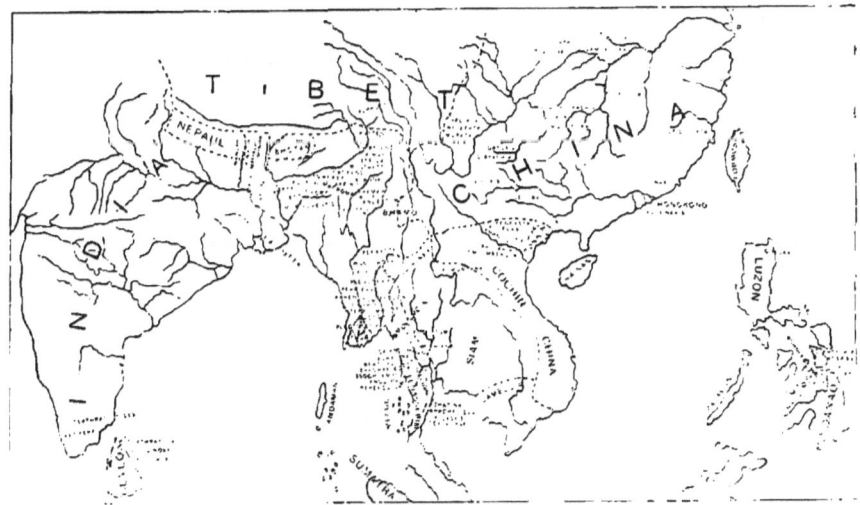

MAP, SHOWING DISTRIBUTION OF GENUS PLECTOPYLIS.

habitats, some curious and striking facts in the distribution of the genus *Plectopylis* become apparent. It will be seen that the centre of distribution appears to be Lower Burma, especially Pegu and Tenasserim; while no species occur to the south-east, the whole of Siam and Cochin China being blanks. Going east the Burmese Shan States and Laos each possess one species, *P. shanensis* and *P. laomontana* respectively, while Tonkin has eight. Upper Burma contributes one species from the Bhamo district, *P. andersoni*, one from Munipur, *P. munipurensis*, and three species in the south, i.e., *P. perarcta*, *P. ponsonbyi*, and *P. woodthorpei*. Assam has fourteen species. Going west we find another blank till we reach Sikkim, the western limit of the genus, where there are five species. The intervening country, Bhutan, has scarcely been explored, but Lieut.-Col. Godwin-Austen, the only naturalist, I

exploration will bring to light many additional species, and possibly both Siam and Cochin China will, when they are searched diligently, be found to possess some interesting forms of the genus.

On page 149 I stated that no fossil forms of Plectopylis are known. I omitted to mention, however, that Dr. Stoliczka described three species of fossil Helices, which he referred to the section Anchistoma Gonostoma, stating that they had affinity with *Plectopylis* and *Corilla*. (Cretaceous Fauna of Southern India, II., p. 9 *et. seq.*). Mr. Nevill, who examined these fossil shells, on the other hand, was of opinion that their appearance did not warrant this theory. (Journ. Asiat. Soc. Beng. L., 1881, p. 128).

I append a key to the species which I venture to hope will prove serviceable ; and for convenience of reference, I have added an index.

I. Section ENDOTHYRA.

A. Palatal folds in one series.
a. Shell 14-15 m.m. horizontal fold below parietal plate .. .. *pinacis.*
b. Shell not exceeding 9 m.m. horizontal fold absent .. .. *sowerbyi.*

B. Palatal folds in two series.
a. Parietal plate without denticles .. *sultani*
b. Parietal plate with one denticle posteriorly .. .. *macromphalus*
c. Parietal plate with two denticles posteriorly.
  α. Shell not exceeding 6 m.m.
    ° One upper and one basal palatal fold.
      † A short horizontal fold above parietal plate .. .. .. *blanda.*
      †† horizontal fold none .. .. *minor.*
    ° ° Only one basal palatal fold *hanleyi.*
  β. shell 8-10 m.m.
    ° Parietal plate gives off anteriorly a horizontal fold from upper extremity ; one short horizontal fold below .. *plectostoma.*
    ° ° No horizontal fold proceeding from parietal plate ; two short horizontal folds below .. .. *affinis.*

II. Section CHERSAECIA.

1. DEXTRAL.

A. Transverse parietal plate simple.
a. Free horizontal parietal folds none.
  α. Palatal folds *six.*
    ° Connected by a transverse ridge ; shell 27 m.m. .. .. *oglei.*
    °° Not connected ; shell 24-26 m.m. .. *andersoni.*
  β. Palatal folds *five* ; shell 11 m.m. .. *serica.*
  γ. Palatal folds *seven* with two denticles *laomontana.*
b. A free interrupted horizontal fold in front of parietal plate ; palatal folds *six,* four inner united by a vertical ridge, seven denticles posteriorly .. .. *austeni.*

B. Transverse parietal plate giving off anteriorly *above* a *short* horizontal fold, with a denticle below plate. Palatal folds *six* ; shell 10-11 m.m. .. .. *munipurensis.*

C. Transverse parietal plate giving off anteriorly *below* a *long* horizontal fold.
a. With a median horizontal fold *continuous* to the peristome ; shell 20 m.m. .. *brachydiscus.*
b. With a median horizontal fold *interrupted* ; shell 16 m.m. .. .. .. *dextrorsa.*

2. SINISTRAL.

Parietal plate simple.
a. Horizontal fold below transverse parietal plate, *short.*
  α. No median fold .. .. .. *insupratti.*
  β. A long median fold present.
    A third short horizontal fold between upper and lower parietal folds.
      † Palatal folds, all horizontal, shell 10 m.m. .. .. *perarcta.*
      †† Palatal folds, one vertical, rest horizontal ; shell 7.5 m.m. .. *shiroiensis.*
    °° No third fold present .. .. *nagaensis.*
b. Horizontal fold below transverse parietal plate long, joined to apertural ridge *perrierae.*
c. Three short horizontal folds in front of transverse parietal plate, none below it *refuga.*

B. Transverse parietal plate giving off anteriorly below a short horizontal fold ; a long median and a long lower fold present, joined to apertural ridge.
a. Palatal folds : all horizontal .. .. *shanensis.*
b. Palatal folds : one oblique, rest horizontal.

α. Parietal plate *rounded* in outline .. *leiophis.*
β. Parietal plate *toothed* in outline .. *pseudophis.*

C. Transverse parietal plate giving off anteriorly below a short horizontal fold, two short free horizontal folds above the latter, and a long one below joining the apertural ridge .. .. *brahma.*

III. Section ENDOPLON.

A. Shell flattened.
a. Armature unknown .. .. .. *phlyaria.*
b. Two vertical parietal plates .. .. *brachyplecta.*
c. One vertical parietal plate with two denticles in front .. .. .. *smithiana.*

B. Shell with more or less conical spire.
a. One transverse parietal plate.
  α. One denticle in front of parietal plate.
    ° Parietal plate rounded in outline ; shell not exceeding 26 m.m. .. *schlumbergeri.*
    °° Parietal plate toothed in outline ; shell. 30 m.m. .. .. .. *jovia.*
  β. Two denticles in front of parietal plate .. .. *villedaryi.*
b. Two transverse parietal plates.
  α. One horizontal parietal fold.
    ° above anterior plate .. .. *giardi.*
    °° below both plates .. .. *congesta.*
  β. Two horizontal parietal folds, one above, one below, the latter joined to the two transverse plates .. .. *frunyaisi.*

IV. Section PLECTOPYLIS, S.S.

A. Two transverse parietal plates.
a. Parietal plates parallel ; upper horizontal palatal fold bisected. Shell less than 20 m.m.
  α. Median parietal fold truncate, not joined to apertural ridge .. *ponsonbyi.*
  β. Median parietal fold not truncate, joined to apertural ridge .. .. *lissochlamys.*
b. Parietal plates divergent ; upper horizontal palatal fold not bisected. Shell more than 20 m.m. .. .. .. *magna.*
c. Anterior parietal plate giving off a long horizontal fold above, and
  α. A short one below, half the length of upper ; palatal folds in two series *woodthorpei.*
  β. Lower fold one-quarter of the length of upper ; palatal folds in one series .. *leucochila.*

B. Three transverse parietal plates.. *feddeni.*

C. Parietal plate ramified.
a. Shell acutely keeled. Parietal fold trifurcate ; a short horizontal fold near aperture .. .. *cyclaspis.*
b. Shell not keeled. Parietal fold trifurcate.
  α. No horizontal fold below parietal plate, a free interrupted horizontal fold in front .. .. *cairnsi.*
  β. Parietal fold giving off anteriorly an interrupted horizontal fold ; a short horizontal fold below plate .. .. *linterae.*
  γ. Parietal fold giving off anteriorly a continuous fold
    ° Shell thin *karenorum.*
    °° Shell thick.
      † Upper arm of parietal fold longest, lower horizontal fold united to apertural ridge .. *repercussa.*
      †† Lower arm longest, lower horizontal fold not united to apertural ridge.
        ‖ Whorls much flattened, umbilicus very shallow .. .. *anguina.*
        ‖) Whorls less flattened, umbilicus deeper .. .. *achatina.*

V. Section SINICOLA.

A. Armature unknown..   ..   ..   *jugatoria.*
                                  alphonsi.
                                  vallata.

B. Two transverse parietal plates.
  a. Shell 6 m.m...   *diptychia.*
  b. Shell 16 m.m.   ..   ..   *biforis.*

C. One transverse parietal plate.
  a. Parietal denticles or folds none.
    a. Palatal folds in one series, parietal
    horizontal fold at aperture.
        * Shell 6.5 m.m.   ..   *invia.*
        ** Shell 9 m.m.   ..   *secura.*
    β. Palatal folds in two series   *schizoptychia*
    No horizontal fold at aperture.
  b. Two parietal denticles anterior to
  transverse plate.
    a. Whorls angular or keeled, palatal
    folds six.
      ᵛ Whorls 4½, shell not exceeding 7 mm.   *emoriens.*
      -ᵛ Whorls 6.
       † Shell 15 m.m...   ..   *fimbriosa.*
       †† Shell 12 m.m.   ..   ..   *azona.*
    β. Whorls rounded, palatal folds 7   ..   *pulvinaris.*
  c. Two parietal denticles posterior to
  transverse plate   ..   ..   ..   *cutisculpta.*
  d. One or two horizontal folds in front of
  parietal plate.
    a. Shell acutely keeled, umbilicus
    moderately deep: two vertical denticles
    between folds   ..   ..   *reserata.*
    β. Shell angulated, umbilicus very deep:
    one horizontal denticle between folds ..   *laminifera.*
  e. Two short horizontal folds in front of
  parietal plate, with one to four denticles
  between.
    a. Shell conical above, 6½ -7 whorls.
      ᵛ Whorls rounded   ..   *stenochila.*
      ᵛᵛ Whorls keeled   ..   v. *basilia.*
    β. Shell depressed, 5½ - 6 whorls   *murata.*
  f. One short horizontal fold above, with
  four or five denticles below, in front of
  parietal plate ; shell shining, pellucid   *multispira.*

VI. Section ENTEROPLAX.

A. Palatal folds : *four.*
  a. Horizontal parietal folds united by a
  vertical ridge posteriorly   ..   *quadrasi.*
  b. Parietal folds not united ..
    a. Umbilicus moderate   *teochospira.*
    β. Umbilicus narrower   ..   v. *boholensis.*
B. Palatal folds : *ten*   ..   ..   ..   *polyptychia.*

VII. Section SYKESIA.

A. *One* transverse parietal fold.
  a. Notched about the middle, a short support posteriorly above. Ceylon.
    a. Umbilicus wide ribs and lyrae
    prominent   ..   ..   *clathratula.*
    β. Umbilicus narrower ribs and lyrae
    obsolete   ..   ..   v. *compressa.*
  b. Not notched.
    a. Straight, without support, umbilicus
    still narrower. Habitat. India ..   *clathratuloides.*
    β. Sinuous, with a short support an-
    teriorly above ; umbilicus still narrower,
    Habitat, India   ..   ..   *retifera.*
B. *Two* transverse parietal plates.
  a. Shell flattened, no fold below umbilical
  angulation, umbilicus still narrower,
  Habitat, Ceylon   ..   ..   *caliginosa.*
  b. Shell conoid, with a double fringe of
  curved hairs ; a horizontal fold below
  umbilical angulation ; umbilicus still
  narrower. Narrowest of all. Hab., Ceylon   *biciliata.*

In concluding this consideration of the genus *Plectopylis*, I desire to acknowledge my indebtedness to many friends and correspondents without whose ungrudging assistance I could not have proceeded with the task. To Mr. Ponsonby I owe an irredeemable debt of gratitude, for in addition to valuable advice and suggestions, he has placed his unrivalled collection at my disposal. Lieut.-Col. Godwin-Austen, Mr. Edgar Smith, and Mr. S. F. Harmer have also placed me under deep obligation ; the first-named communicated undescribed material, and all have allowed me access to type specimens. Miss Linter has very obligingly presented me with a series of shells, some of which proved to be new, while finally- for the loan of specimens from their collections, or from collections under their charge—I have to thank Prof. Boettger, Col. Beddome, the Rev. R. A. Bullen, Mr. W. T. Blanford, Mr. Robert Cairns, Mr. W. E. Collinge, the Rev. Vincenz Gredler, Mr. H. Fulton, Dr. H. Fischer, Prof. Giard, Mr. E. L. Layard, Mr. Jules Mabille, Prof. von Martens, Dr. von Möllendorff, Dr. F. J. H. Merrill, Mr. E. R. Sykes, and Mr. G. B. Sowerby. To the Editor of SCIENCE GOSSIP, I am also greatly indebted for his unremitting courtesy, attention to details, and for affording space in the pages of this Magazine, frequently, I fear, to the exclusion of matter more interesting to the general readers.

Adelaide Road. London, N.W.
 2nd September, 1899.

www.ingramcontent.com/pod-product-compliance
Lightning Source LLC
Chambersburg PA
CBHW020046030726
47499CB00007B/2601